Sixteen

Poppy Kinsey was convinced there were three-legged tortoises and hibernating sloths that moved faster than her friend. Freya was walking even more slowly than usual – and that was saying something. One foot scuffed achingly in front of the other. It occurred to Poppy that plodding footsteps were more or less the soundtrack of their friendship.

One thing Freya *did* have over tortoises and sloths, though, was multi-tasking. Her left hand was hoisting a shopping bag as her right tapped out a one-thumbed text message at dizzying speed. That was something at which she *was* an expert. She'd taken opposable thumbs to a new level of evolution.

Freya's boyfriend, Mark, turned and gave Poppy a knowing half-smile.

Yeah, I know, he didn't say.

Freya muttered something to Mark that Poppy didn't catch and then re-pocketed the phone. Her pace didn't increase and Poppy had known her friend for long enough to suspect there was something going on.

'This bag's too heavy,' Freya moaned, holding it a little higher and offering it to Mark.

'I'm not an octopus,' he replied. 'I only have two hands – and they're both carrying your shopping already. There are three pairs of shoes in these bags. Three! Who needs three new pairs of shoes?'

Freya rarely took no for an answer. She held the bag higher until Mark snatched it away. He lumbered the rest of her bags onto his opposite shoulder and started waddling like a tipsy emperor penguin.

Poppy trailed behind them along the pavement, feeling tiny beads of sweat beginning to pool on her forehead. It was the final day of July and the sun was sitting high among the vast expanse of blue sky. She swished her top, hoping the sweat wasn't going to create a damp patch.

This was how they had spent so many days this summer: Mark and Freya side by side, Poppy following like a forlorn puppy. She was never quite sure if she minded. Most of the time she didn't, but every now and then, even though she tried to bury it, she experienced a pang of jealousy that their trio was a two-plus-one.

She was the one.

It had been a dull hour on the bus, travelling the thirty miles from the centre of Bristol as it dropped its inhabitants off into the surrounding leafy towns and parishes. Mobile reception came and went and the crush of passengers had sent the temperature soaring. Poppy was relieved to be home in their village of Purley.

The three of them mooched away from the village centre, heading across the neatly trimmed green towards the medieval church. Flowers blossomed around the edges of the green and the smell of freshly cut grass clung to the air.

They crossed the cobbled bridge painfully slowly and then Freya stopped and nodded at the stone building that ran alongside the River Purley.

'Didn't you say you needed the loo, Mark?'

Mark stared at her for a second too long before his eyebrows shot up. 'Right, yeah. Be right back.'

He dropped the shopping bags on the pavement and scuttled off towards the toilets.

Poppy watched him go, trying to figure out what she'd missed. Freya's deathly slow march was bad enough, but even more frustrating was the fact that the entire journey back had been punctuated by silent conversations between the couple. They had spoken with widened eyes, raised eyebrows and gentle tilts of the head.

They were the strangest of couples. Mark was tall, athletic and lean with short dark hair and a natural ability for, well, everything. Freya, on the other hand, was shorter and wider, with big hips, a curvy backside and curvier chest that had appeared from nowhere three summers ago. Boys seemed to have a thing for curves at their age. Freya put it all down to her mother's Jamaican heritage, which seemed more likely than it coming from her father. He'd disappeared back to whatever corner of London he'd come from when she was still a toddler.

Unlike Mark, Freya's thing was definitely not academia – though what she lacked in ability, she tried to make up for with enthusiasm.

And volume. Her range consisted of loud and louder.

'What's going on with you two?' Poppy asked.

Freya replied too quickly: 'What? Nothing's going on.'

'You keep looking at each other… weirdly.'

'No, we don't.' Freya flicked her hair backwards with both of her hands, not trying to hide the change of subject. 'We should go shopping in Bristol more often.'

'You say that every time your mum gives you money – then you spend it all in one go. Like today.'

Freya picked up one of the bags. 'Yeah, but did you see my shoes? They're so pretty, Pops. They should open a Primark here. Better than all these stupid cottages and grass.'

Poppy turned to look at the centre of the village. As well as the church and green, there was a war memorial on the other side of the road, plus a row of thatched-roofed cottages that had been there for hundreds of years.

It was like living in a postcard.

'I'm not sure you'd get that past the council,' Poppy said.

Freya pushed herself up onto the tips of her toes, bobbing up and down. She wasn't one for standing still; she constantly fidgeted as if she had somewhere else to be. 'Maybe I'll stand for council,' she said. 'How old have you got to be? Eighteen? That's only a year and a bit away – I'd be great. I'd get us a McDonald's, a Primark, a Topshop, plus a Nando's.'

'You reckon people would vote for you?'

'You'd vote for me – and Mark. That's two. Mum too, I reckon.'

'You'll need more than three votes.'

Freya waved a finger in Poppy's face. 'You don't reckon they'd vote for a black girl round here? You saying they're racist?'

Poppy opened her mouth to answer and then realised Freya had cracked into a grin. 'Tell you what,' Poppy said, '*if* you stand for council, I'll vote for you.'

'You saying I won't?'

Poppy linked her arm through Freya's. 'I *know* you won't. By the time we're eighteen, we'll be off at uni and this place will be a long way away.'

Freya didn't reply because she had her phone out of her pocket again and was checking the screen. She tapped something and then put it away. Considering the only two people with whom Freya hung around were already with her, Poppy had no idea what she was up to.

And then, all of a sudden, she knew.

It seemed so blindingly obvious that she couldn't believe she'd missed it. Freya usually wanted to go shopping when she got her monthly allowance – but always on the same day. Month after month, the three of them ended up in the city on a Saturday. This time, for some reason, Freya had told Poppy they had to go on Sunday instead. They'd got up early to catch the bus because the shops weren't open as long on Sundays. Given that Freya could barely haul herself into school by nine in the morning, it was more than strange for her to have suggested this.

'You all right?' Freya asked.

Poppy blinked back onto the bridge, realising Freya was talking to her. 'Um…'

'You spaced out for a minute.'

Poppy's throat was dry as she tried to swallow, wanting to convince herself that she'd got it wrong. 'I'm fine,' she said.

'So what d'you reckon?' Freya added, and Poppy realised she'd missed part of a conversation.

'You're right,' she said, figuring it was as good a reply as any.

'Damn right I am. We're both sixteen – it's just cos she's so old. We had a right row about it last night. I was like, "Why can't Mark stay over? It's not like we have to worry about our GCSEs now." Then my mum was like, "I'm not having that going on under my roof." I was like, "Maybe I'll get a roof of my own." Then she was like, "You do that." The cow. She's just jealous.'

Before Poppy could reply, Mark emerged from the toilets, wiping his hands on his shorts. He picked up the shopping bags with a smile and nod for Freya, and they continued along the dusty paths that led away from the centre of the village.

Purley Hill steepled over them: a long, straight road arching up and away from the village. Trees lined both sides, dousing all below in a cooling shadow that took the edge off the balminess of the day. Poppy, Freya and Mark passed into the shade and then turned to take the path that hugged the edge of the river.

They were heading towards Poppy's house but Freya was moving at an even more leisurely pace than before. She was scuffing her feet, swinging her free arm, complaining to anyone who'd listen – which was nobody – that her legs were sore from the shopping trip. If she moved any more slowly, she'd be going backwards.

What should have been a five-minute walk took almost fifteen. Eventually, they emerged from an alley onto the road where Poppy lived. There was a line of houses set back from the road, each with small gardens at the front and huge ones at the back.

The trio was just about to cross the road when Freya stepped away from Mark and dropped her handbag. It thumped onto the ground, the top flying open as the contents of the Boots make-up counter spilled onto the tarmac. Freya gasped, 'Oops,' then dropped to her knees and started to repack everything. She tugged on Mark's trousers, asking him to help, but Poppy stood where she was, staring towards her house. The road was usually clear except for a handful of cars, but there was now a row of a dozen or so vehicles.

'You should have told me,' she whispered.

'Huh?'

Poppy looked down at Freya, who was trying to act as if everything was fine. Her sideways glance towards Mark gave her up once and for all.

Without waiting for them, Poppy dashed across the road. Mark called after her, but Poppy bounded along the pavement, then the driveway, up to her front door. In a flash, the key was in her hand and she stumbled into the gloom.

The hallway was the darkest part of the house and would be shrouded in permanent dusk if they didn't leave the living room door open. It was *always* open, allowing daylight to eat into the murk.

The door was closed.

Poppy thought about turning and heading back to the centre of Purley. She had lived in the village her entire life. As much as she couldn't wait to get away, it was her playground. She knew the lanes, trails and cut-throughs; the hidey-holes to shelter from the rain; the secluded fields to bathe in the sun. If she ran now, she could find a spot where nobody would bother her. It would be better than walking into what was on the other side of the door.

How *could* they? Freya, Mark, her father – they knew what today was.

Poppy turned and took a step back towards the front door – but Mark was suddenly there, sweating and out of breath as he dropped Freya's shopping bags on the doorstep.

'What's wrong?' he panted.

Poppy didn't think he'd done it on purpose, but he had blocked her in her own hallway. The bright sunlight dazzled behind him, silhouetting his slender figure in the doorframe.

Freya's shape appeared over Mark's shoulder as she hunched over, hands on knees. 'Girl! You can really run.'

Poppy had nowhere to go. She found herself sucked into the darkness of the hall, drifting to the far end, knowing what was going to happen. She pulled down the cool metal handle and pushed, took one step forward and then—

'SURPRIIIIIIIIIIIIIIIISE!'

Poppy blinked.

Her living room was filled with people: kids from school, neighbours, one or two of her dad's friends, a few people from the village. They all smiled and cheered expectantly. Her dad was front and centre, beaming. The walls were decorated with rainbow streamers and banners. So much colour.

Freya elbowed her way around Poppy into the living room. 'I think she guessed,' she said, nudging Poppy's father with her arm. 'She's a smart one, Mr K. It weren't my fault – I didn't say nothing.'

Poppy stared at them, gulping back the lump in her throat.

'Happy birthday, Pops,' her father said, making a move towards her.

Before he could reach her, Poppy turned, pushing past Mark and making a run for it. There was a babbling of voices behind her but she charged through the front door, spun at the end of the driveway and blazed past the row of cars, sprinting for the end of the road. She didn't know where she was going, just that she couldn't be in the house with all those people. She had been worried about sweating through her top, but she didn't care any longer. Poppy ran and ran, moving so quickly that it felt like her legs were going faster than the rest of her body. She'd race off the edge of a cliff in cartoon style, hang in mid-air and then plummet.

She darted onto the track that skirted the house at the furthest end of the road, ducking under the clawing branches of an apple tree and feeling the welcome chill. Suddenly, she was trembling. She wrapped her arms around her sweat-stained top as she slowed to a walk. The gravel crunched underfoot and Poppy's eyes spun with purple and green stars at the sudden change of light. She stumbled ahead to the crossroads, where the shingle trail intersected with a crumbling dirt lane.

Poppy stopped to catch her breath, only then realising there were tears dribbling down her cheeks. She breathed in deeply through her nose, trying to compose herself as she dried her eyes with the bottom of her T-shirt.

In through the nose, out through the mouth. Calm.

She was on the lane that flanked the back gardens of her row of houses. She turned and started to walk towards the gate at the back of her house, still dabbing her eyes. The last few minutes had been a blur and she wasn't entirely sure how it had all happened. In the moment she'd seen all those people in her house, she'd known she had to get away.

Why had her dad done it? It was her birthday – but so much more than that. Since the previous year, July the thirty-first was always going to have a second meaning.

Poppy felt *silly*. Embarrassed. Regardless of anything else, all those people had just seen her run out of the house like a *silly* child. These were people who'd known her all her life – and she'd humiliated herself in front of them all. In a village where everyone knew everyone else, that was some going. She'd have to stay in her room for the rest of the summer, if only to avoid their pity-filled stares.

It was all her dad's fault.

Poppy stood on tiptoes to peer over the top of her back gate. From what she could see, there was nobody in the back garden and, although there were dark shapes silhouetted through the windows at the rear of the house, nobody appeared to be watching. Poppy stretched her arm through the gap between the gate and the post and reached for the latch. She'd first taught herself this trick when she was five or six.

Poppy felt like that little girl again now. She creaked the gate open and edged into the garden. She could have run and run; could have found herself a spot in the woods outside the village and hid. But as annoyed as she was with her father, she needed to be at home.

She skirted the line of the hedge until she reached the tree in the back corner of the garden. It had grown with her, from a sapling that had once matched her height, to the faithful shelter it now provided. When her dad was at work and there was no Freya or Mark to keep her company, Poppy would sometimes sit under that tree. If she was in the mood, she'd draw in her sketchbook; other times, she'd read or play with her phone.

After a final glance towards the house, Poppy wedged herself against the trunk, using it to shield her from anyone inside. The rough bark pressed into her back as she clasped her knees to her chest and closed her eyes, listening. More than anything, this was what she liked doing on this spot. She'd close her eyes and tune in to the sounds of the village. She could hear them now – friends, neighbours, *everyone* – whispering about her. Tittering to one another, asking if they'd heard about the crazy, *silly* girl who'd run out of her own birthday party.

'Pops.'

Poppy opened her eyes to see her father standing in front of her. He had his hands in his pockets; the top few buttons of his polo shirt were undone. He was smiling kindly, dark eyes twinkling. Despite the anger Poppy wanted to feel towards him, the fury she wanted to throw at him, it wasn't there.

'Hi,' she croaked.

'You OK?'

Poppy nodded and her dad creaked his way down until he was sitting next to her, his back also pressed against the trunk. He grunted as a click echoed around the garden.

'Knees aren't what they were,' he said.

Poppy closed her eyes again.

'How'd you know I'd be here?' Poppy asked.

'I guessed.'

'I'm that predictable, hey?'

She felt his hand on top of hers. It was warm but not from the heat of the day. 'I'm sorry,' he said. 'This was my idea – I should've known better. I know what today is, but I thought we should do something special for your sixteenth birthday.'

He paused and there was a wonderful moment of silence punctuated only by the chirping of a bird somewhere off in the distance. When he spoke again, his voice was quieter. 'It's your day, too.'

Poppy squeezed her eyes closed so tightly that they hurt. It meant she couldn't cry. 'It's Mum's day,' she managed.

Her father's hand tightened on hers and Poppy let it. She could feel him looking at her but didn't dare open her eyes.

'I miss your mother, too,' he said. 'But your life can't be defined by somebody else's death, no matter whose it is. The fact that your mum died on your birthday is a coincidence, a horrible piece of chance – but still a fluke.'

Poppy didn't know how to reply. Any words would stick in her throat. She felt her father brushing away a strand of loose hair from her face. It had been a year since that horrible day in the hospital. Twelve months. Three hundred and sixty-five days. Sometimes, Poppy thought she was over it; other times…

Poppy's father squeezed her hand again. 'Let's go back to the party,' he said.

Poppy's eyes were aching so much that she couldn't keep them closed any longer. When she opened them, the tears she'd been fighting flooded down her cheeks. The lump that was in her throat released itself with a gasp.

'They're still here?' she asked.

Poppy's father nodded... or at least, that's what it looked like through the mask of tears. 'They're waiting for you.'

'Everyone will think I'm a silly kid.'

'They won't. They've known you forever. They understand.'

Poppy wasn't sure she wanted them to understand. They *should* think she was a silly kid, because that was how she felt. Sixteen going on six.

'I think I need a few minutes,' she whispered.

'Nobody's going anywhere for a while – you've got presents to open. And there's cake. I got it from Mrs Rawtenstall. She made it specially.'

'I told you, I'm not eating carbs.'

He laughed, dismissive but kind. 'It's your birthday, Pops. You can have some cake.'

Poppy didn't want to argue. Did icing have carbs in it? Probably. Everything good had carbs in it.

Her father's grip on her hand loosened. 'I've got something for you,' he said. His tone had changed slightly. He sounded nervous.

'What?'

'I wasn't sure when to give it to you. It's something special. It's probably best if you have it after everyone's gone.'

She tugged at the top he'd given her that morning. Poppy had picked it but he'd paid for it and put it away.

'Another present?' she asked.

'Sort of,' he replied, but Poppy couldn't read his face. He scratched his chin and then grumbled his way up until he was standing, clutching at his lower back.

'I thought it was your knees that had gone?' Poppy said.

'When you get to my age, Pops, everything goes.'

Afternoon became evening and the visitors to Poppy's house slowly drifted back to their own homes. Nobody had said anything about her escapade but words weren't always necessary. The slight tilt of their heads and the searching gazes were enough. It was as if all they wanted to do was put their collective arms around her and say it would be fine. Lots of people had been saying that for the past year. She'd heard the word 'fine' more than any other.

Thankfully, nobody tried to put their arms around her this time. They could keep their pity.

Poppy had ended up with quite a birthday haul. It was mainly the type of generic stuff all teenagers got. If Poppy was honest, all she'd wanted was money. Sixteen-year-olds did not have money, because they were too busy faffing around with things like exams. The adults had, instead, handed over various vouchers and an assortment of smelly stuff that Poppy didn't really want. She was too polite to show anything other than gratefulness, however. Only Mark had put in any real thought, giving her a set of twenty coloured pencils in a tin from which she would definitely get some use. Freya had given some book vouchers, although Poppy was fairly sure this was a re-gift of the same vouchers Freya had been given the previous Christmas.

She let it go. It was what they did.

Finally, the house was empty except for Poppy and her father. Poppy sat in the large armchair with a large bowl of fluorescent green jelly in her lap. It wibbled and wobbled as she jabbed at it with a spoon.

'I can't believe you made jelly,' she said.

Her father was on the sofa, eating a Jaffa Cake. 'Are there carbs in jelly?' he asked with a grin.

Poppy lifted an overloaded, barely balanced spoonful to her mouth. 'Who cares?' She swallowed the lot and delved for more. She didn't know what it was supposed to taste of, other than 'green'. Green was a flavour, right?

As she ate, her father crossed to the bureau in the far corner of the living room. It was where he kept his passport and other important documents. Forever locked and out-of-bounds. She watched as he unlatched the top drawer and took out something rectangular and cream-coloured. He walked across the room and placed the object on the arm of Poppy's chair. She put down her spoon, eyes widening as she spotted the handwriting on the front of the envelope.

Poppy

Her name was written in a swished spiral of swirls. Poppy looked up to her dad, who had returned to the sofa. 'Mum's handwriting,' she said. It wasn't a question.

Poppy's dad nodded slowly, hands clasped in front of him, as if in prayer. He didn't seem to know what to do with himself, shifting his weight from hip to hip. It was several moments before he spoke. 'Your mother knew she was ill and what was going to happen to her. She gave me that the day before she was taken to hospital and made me promise to give it to you on your sixteenth birthday.'

'What's inside?'

He shook his head. 'I don't know. She never told me and I didn't ask. It's between you and her.'

Poppy moved the bowl of jelly to the side and picked up the envelope, staring at her name on the front. The paper was thick, not quite card, and rippled with some sort of watermark. It felt expensive.

'Pops,' her dad whispered.

'What?'

'There are more: one for each of your next nine birthdays. She wanted to find a way of remaining in your life…'

Poppy swallowed, turning the envelope over in her hand. The flap on the back was sealed with a sliver of dark brown paper, woven into a pretty bow. This must have been one of the last things her mother had done.

'I didn't know if it was a good idea to give it to you,' her dad continued. 'I've had that all year, wondering what I should do. In the end, I realised it's not my decision.'

Poppy nodded, turning the envelope back over again and running her thumb across the pen marks. She wanted to see what was inside, but at the same time, she didn't.

Her mother always wrote beautifully: flowing, joined-up letters that were so intricate they barely seemed like words. Poppy had inherited none of that talent.

She flipped the envelope and scratched the bow with her fingernail until it came loose.

'You don't have to do this, Pops,' her father said.

She looked up, meeting his gaze. 'I want to.'

The flap of the envelope lifted and Poppy reached inside, pulling out two folded sheets made of the same expensive paper as the envelope. She took a breath and unfurled the pages, then said she was going to her room.

My dearest Poppy,

I've wondered for a long time whether I should do this. That this might be a selfish act because I want to somehow live on in your life. I honestly don't know any longer. I've started this letter a dozen times and then screwed it up and began again.

If you choose not to read on, I'll understand. You shouldn't feel burdened by me, but then, I suppose the reason I'm writing – I hope the reason I'm writing – is that there are going to be so many things I wish I could've told you in person. I won't get the chance to do that, so perhaps this is my best shot.

One of the things I've worried about for the longest time is whether a daughter will automatically turn into her mother. It's a fear I've had because I never wanted to be like my mum.

I'd like to think I've been my own person – but secrecy in my family has always been a way of life. As you know, I was raised solely by my mum, and the only thing she ever told me about my father was that he joined the army, was stationed abroad, and – like too many young men – never came back.

The only life I ever knew her to have was the one she lived at home with me. It wasn't until after her death that I discovered she'd had a job – a career, even. I was clearing out some of her old things and found a small, crumpled stack of these old programmes. They had addresses from London theatres, with cast lists from plays and musicals. She used to be an organist, something I didn't know until it was too late. I never saw her take an interest in music.

I was raised to keep my feelings to myself and have spent a lifetime doing that. There's so much you don't know about me. I'm not strong enough, nor will I have enough time, to rectify that in person. Perhaps these letters will help to change things.

I may as well start somewhere near the beginning, with my mother – your grandmother. I know you never met and, though you've asked questions, I've not told you very much about her. That's because – and this is hard to write – I'm not sure that she was a nice person.

She expected perfection in everything. For instance, when I was at primary school, everyone in my year was entered into a handwriting competition. It was an annual thing that we all knew was coming. We were each given a Rudyard Kipling poem to read and then transcribe, using our joined-up handwriting skills. I'd been practising for weeks. Thinking about the number of hours I put into it now makes me shiver – especially because some sod popped up and invented personal computers, so nobody uses pens any longer!

There was a time limit, but I finished and had enough time to look back over my work. It was as faultless as anything I'd ever done. Perfect curves, straight lines, elaborate loops – everything I'd slaved over.

We got the results in an assembly a few days later. I'd come second in the year. Some lad named Isaac Connolly won. I can still picture him now, wearing these little grey shorts as he went up to get the award. He had this mop of blond hair, like an angel-faced choirboy. I was staring at him, thinking, 'You little so-and-so' – but really, I was devastated because I knew what was awaiting me.

When I got home, my mother asked how it went. I showed her my certificate saying I came second, and she tutted. She didn't speak to me properly for three days after that.

I was never smacked, never hit or clipped or anything like that – even though that sort of thing was common at the time. Instead, it was day after day of small punishments, that somehow were so much worse than getting it all over with at once.

The strangest thing was that, at the time, I was OK with it all. I didn't know any differently. It is only as I've got older that I've thought back to everything and seen it in a new light. Even now, I wonder whether she was so strict because she wanted me to be the best I could be, or because she genuinely didn't like me.

That's something I will never know.

But it did affect so many things in my life. When I was sixteen – which wasn't 'in the Stone Age', as you once told me – my friends used to push their bikes to the top of Purley Hill and then race to the bottom. I never did, partly because I was scared, but also because I thought my mother would disapprove. I didn't want to seem silly in front of her, or my friends. Now, as I lie here, I really wish I'd done it with them anyway. It seemed like so much fun, then and now. I can still hear my friends laughing as they zoomed to the bottom.

Now you've turned sixteen, the important thing is that your life is your life. Embrace it and relish it, because life is a gift that is supposed to be enjoyed.

Us adults are frequently suspicious of the young. You see it all the time on the news, hear the whispers on the streets. It's always seen as such a terrible thing that young people are gathering with their friends, wearing strange clothes, saying words we've never heard, listening to music we don't like.

We forget so quickly that you're us and we're you.

We were all sixteen once. You should never underestimate the power of simply having fun – especially at your age, before the boring adult stuff catches you up. Trust me, dragging yourself around

IKEA on a Sunday afternoon is not enjoyable, nor is sitting around filling in an insurance application form!

I'm so sorry I can't be there to see you blossom. I love you very much. Happy birthday.

Mum

Poppy didn't leave her room for much of the evening. She read the letter five times, with each go-over somehow making it feel as if there was a line or two she'd missed before. She returned the pages to the envelope each time, slipping it under her pillow and telling herself she wouldn't read it again – before going through the whole thing over and over.

Time passed, she wasn't sure how long, and then there was a gentle knock on her door. Poppy mumbled something that tried to be 'come in' but it came out as a throaty sob. Her father entered and said nothing as he crossed to sit on the bed at Poppy's side. He put an arm around her and pulled her onto his shoulder. They stayed like that as more time passed.

'Your mother meant well,' her father said eventually, 'but ten years is a long time…'

Poppy pulled herself away and rubbed her eyes. She suddenly realised there were nine more envelopes on the bed at her father's side. She'd somehow missed him bringing them in. Each had her name swirled onto the front.

'It hurts,' Poppy croaked.

'I know, Pops.' He paused, sniffed, and then added: 'Sometimes, you know in advance that something's going to hurt but you do it anyway because it's still worth it.'

Poppy reached around him and picked up an envelope that had a small '22' etched onto the corner.

'You can read them all now if you want,' he said. 'Or not read any of them at all.'

Poppy took another of the envelopes – '17' this time. She thumbed the catch on the back.

'I don't know what to do,' she said quietly.

'Me neither, Pops,' her father replied. 'It's not for me to decide.'

Seventeen

Poppy unlocked her front door and pushed quickly into the hallway, glad to finally be getting a respite from the heat of the day.

'Wasn't your birthday scorchio last year, too?' Mark asked, following her inside.

She closed the door behind him and wiped the crown of sweat from her hairline, hoping he hadn't noticed. Thankfully, he was too busy taking off his shoes. Poppy squeezed around him and headed for the kitchen.

'The universe is celebrating the day of my birth by dousing us in the fire of nine-hundred-and-ninety-nine suns,' she said.

'Why not a thousand?'

'I'm not greedy.'

Poppy dumped her college bag on the side and opened the fridge. She turned and leaned back into the space, enjoying the flood of cool air. Mark shunted himself nearby, resting against her hip. He'd not had his hair cut since their Easter break, and it was the longest Poppy had ever seen it. It was down to his jawline and had a natural curl. The peppering of stubble – that Poppy and Freya had so relentlessly teased him about when it had first appeared three years previously – had become darker and rougher in recent months. It had happened so quickly: one day, Mark had been the lad she'd known most of her life, the butt of her jokes, Freya's boyfriend. Then, from nowhere, he had become a man.

'Shift up,' Mark said.

'It's my fridge. I get first dibs on the cold.'

'You don't own the cold.'

'I own *this* cold.' Poppy bumped him with her hip and he moved across to the sink, grinning. 'What are you smiling about?' she asked.

'Thinking of Frey sitting in class in this weather. She's fuming.'

'I don't understand why college is still open. It's the very end of July. Isn't there a law against that?'

He shrugged. 'At least it's not *us* that has to do summer catch-up classes.'

'Does she still make you get the bus in with her every morning?'

'I wouldn't say she *makes* me…'

'But it's less hassle if you do?'

They exchanged knowing smiles. Poppy had known Freya since they were six years old. That was well enough to know there would have been hell to pay if Mark didn't get the bus with her each morning, whether or not he had to go to college himself. As it happened, all three of them had had to visit the college that morning – it was only Freya who'd had to stay on for the afternoon.

Poppy finally relinquished the fridge, taking out a can of Coke and allowing Mark to rest his back against the cold. She pushed herself up to sit on the counter-top and downed a third of the can in one.

'Your dad at work?' Mark asked.

'What gave it away? The fact he's not here?'

'I should be a detective.'

'He's in London – down and back in a day on the train. Won't be back till late.'

Mark nodded, opening his mouth to reply but then stopping himself. He closed the fridge and there was a moment of awkwardness in which neither of them knew what to say. The kitchen momentarily felt chilly, like the whole room was an open fridge door.

'You want something to eat?' Poppy asked quickly, to break the silence.

As if it had never disappeared, Mark's smile returned. 'I was wondering when you'd ask.'

They hunted through the cupboards until they'd amassed a pile of potential sandwich fillings. Soon, they were standing side by side in a two-person assembly line. Poppy did the buttering and smearing, Mark lumped anything and seemingly everything in between the bread slices. They were eventually left with a selection of sandwiches that no human beings had likely tried before.

Mark bit into sandwich number one, putting a brave face on it as he swallowed.

'What did you get?' Poppy asked.

'I think it's the one with Marmite, peanut butter, lettuce and tomato.'

Poppy winced and then bit into her own, chewing and readying herself for a vicious twist that never came. She nodded approvingly.

'What's yours?' Mark asked.

'Jam, chocolate spread and pickle.'

'You know we're geniuses, don't you?' he said. 'If Jamie Oliver had come up with this, he'd make millions.'

Poppy had another bite of the sandwich. It was even better than the first. They *were* geniuses.

'If we'd done this yesterday,' she said, 'I could've told Mr Stevens this morning that I'm going to be a chef.'

'Stinky Stevens?'

She laughed, but shook her head. 'I don't know why people call him that – he doesn't stink.'

'Yeah, but nicknames have to either rhyme or alliterate. If you're going to have a last name that begins with the letter "S", you're going to have to accept that you might get called stinky.'

Poppy tried to think of something clever that either rhymed or was alliterative with Mark's last name of Ellery. Nothing came to mind.

'Minging Mark,' he said.

'Huh?'

'That's what you were trying to think of.'

'No, I wasn't.'

He grinned. 'So what did you tell our careers officer?'

'That I didn't know what I wanted to be. He said it was getting a bit late.' Poppy swirled her hand around. 'Blah, blah, blah. It's summer, we're supposed to be off – and what's a drop-in session, anyway?'

'Something you drop into?'

'I was being rhetorical.'

Mark had another bite of his sandwich. 'I'm not convinced Marmite and peanut butter works at all.'

'You made your bed and now you have to lie in it.'

'Actually, I made a sandwich.'

'And now you have to, er, lie in it.' Poppy had another taste of her own. Jam, pickle and chocolate spread *definitely* worked.

Mark nodded at the mess in front of them. Breadcrumbs littered the counter-top and the stove, with filling-smeared knives cluttered in the sink. A smudge of peanut butter had somehow ended up on the wall and there were tomato pips on the floor. It looked like a sandwich bomb had gone off.

'You could be a cleaner when you grow up,' he said.

'*You* could be a cleaner.'

'It's your kitchen. You can't monopolise the fridge cold on the basis of living here and then abdicate responsibility when it comes to cleaning up.'

'You're the one who got peanut butter on the wall.'

Mark put his sandwich down, tucked a loose strand of hair behind his ear and scratched his sandpaper chin. He reached across her, slipping the sketchbook out of her bag from where it lay on the countertop. He opened the cover of the book, his features now more serious. His jaw was straight and fixed, lips no longer smiling.

'Why didn't you tell Stinky Stevens you wanted to be an artist?' he asked.

Poppy turned away, not wanting to see his reaction to her work, not really wanting him to be looking at all. It would be too much to tug the pad away, though.

She shrugged. 'I did.'

'What did he say?'

'That I needed something to fall back on. That drawing was a hobby.'

Mark looked up, but she avoided his gaze by biting into her sandwich and staring at the peanut butter mark on the wall.

'People make a living from art,' he said.

She chewed and chewed, until she couldn't get away with it any longer. '*Good* people do.'

'You're good.'

She shrugged again. 'I'll come up with something. We're not all like you.'

He returned the book to her bag. 'What d'you mean?'

'You've always been into computers, always been smart. You'll never need summer classes. You'll be one of those tech geeks like Mark Zuckerberg or Steve Jobs. You'll come up with some amazing idea and make a bazillion pounds.'

'That's not even a number.'

'So you'll invent it. You'll have a huge house, servants, pools, porcupines…'

'Why would I want a porcupine?'

Poppy bit her bottom lip and then burst out laughing. '*Concubines.*'

Mark snickered too. 'I don't think I will.'

'Fine – maybe *you* can be a cleaner then.'

He laughed louder and she did too.

She still wished he hadn't looked through her book, though. It contained work for her art class, yes – but it was personal.

Mark had one more bite and then put his sandwich on the side. 'I think this needs to go in the bin,' he said.

She nodded at the sink. 'Under there. You can tidy up while you're at it.'

As it was, they cleaned together in the same, companionable way they'd made the mess together. Poppy used the mini vacuum and then squirted some surface spray; Mark did the scrubbing. That done, they headed into the living room. Poppy slumped on the sofa and flicked on the television, searching through the music channels until she found something almost agreeable. Mark was in the armchair, satchel at his feet as he fiddled with his phone.

This was something of a pattern that had been continuing since college had broken up. They'd go to each other's houses if there was nobody else home, or else find a spot in the park where they wouldn't be bothered. If Freya was off, the three of them would go for a burger somewhere close to college, or spend hours aimlessly shuffling around shops.

'Is your dad still going on about you getting a summer job?' Poppy asked.

'He's still saying I should be paying rent. He reckons my uncle needs help on his farm. I told him it's my last summer of freedom.'

'What did he say?'

'That if it's my last summer of freedom, why am I spending it bumming around all day?'

Their eyes met and they both started laughing. 'Bumming around' did sum up what they'd spent the summer doing so far.

'When have you got to go back for Frey?' Poppy asked.

'Gotta get the three o'clock bus. You coming?'

'Probably not.'

'Sandwich recipes to work on?'

'Exactly.'

It was then that Mark spotted the envelope on the shelf behind Poppy. It was probably the swirly handwriting on the front that caught his eye. The top of his nose wrinkled as he nodded towards it. 'What's that?'

Poppy didn't need to turn to know what he was referring to. It was the letter from her mum. Number two of ten. Her father had left it out but she'd not wanted to open it. Not yet. Perhaps not at all.

'Are you all right?' Mark added.

'Huh?'

He was staring directly at her, all big brown eyes, soft tan, solid jaw and high cheekbones. 'None of my business.'

Poppy felt herself squirming, unable to escape his gaze. 'I've, um… got a bit of a headache,' she lied.

For a moment he said nothing, stare still fixed. Then, mercifully, he turned away. 'It'll be the sugar rush from the jam and chocolate spread.'

'And it's so hot out.'

'Oh, don't you start.'

'What?'

Mark flung his arms wide towards the window. 'The minute summer comes round, all the old people start going on about their gardens and the plants. We wait all year for this weather, then, when it's here, everyone wants it to go away again. It's like Christmas. It's all presents, food and TV specials, then by six o'clock, everyone's like, "Thank goodness that's done for another year".'

'My dad was talking about the garden yesterday, saying it was too dry.'

'See!'

Poppy didn't want to smile but she couldn't stop herself. Then Mark was smiling too and everything was all right again, the invented headache forgotten by them both.

Mark scratched his chin with his thumb, bristling the thin cover of stubble. He often did this; Poppy wondered if it was because he couldn't quite believe he was old enough to grow a proper beard.

'What did you get for your birthday?' he asked.

'Not much.'

'You must've got something from your dad?'

'Driving lessons. The usual.'

Mark's raised eyebrow told a story of its own.

'I'm not going to do a Frey,' Poppy added, defensively.

'I didn't say a word.'

'She's *your* girlfriend – you should be sticking up for her.'

Mark nodded in agreement, though the upturned corner of his lips disagreed.

'OK,' Poppy added. 'What did she tell you happened?'

Mark plumped up the cushion behind him, relaxing back, ready for story time.

'Well,' he said, 'apparently, it was her third driving lesson and the instructor was so impressed by her natural ability that he was talking about putting her in for her test within weeks.'

'Sounds plausible. Although she told me within *days*.'

Mark's grin was spreading. 'Frey was going round this roundabout when, literally out of thin air, this "crazed old biddy" – that's a direct quote – indicated left, turned right, and cut across Frey. In a moment of driving that Lewis Hamilton would've been proud of, Frey swerved to avoid the out-of-control vehicle, simultaneously avoiding a collision with six pedestrians and every other car on the roundabout.'

'She told me it was four pedestrians.'

'When I first heard the story, it was three, then it was four. As of yesterday, there were six. Next week, it could be a dozen. Anyway, after managing to not hit any of those and veering round a bus—'

'A bus?!'

'That's what she said.'

'I heard a van. Nothing about a bus.'

'Who knows? Either way, she took evasive action, missing the pedestrians and a van disguised as a bus. In doing so, she *momentarily* mounted the kerb. In most circumstances, this would have been manageable for a driver of her ability, except for a shocking lack of maintenance on the kerb. Because of an appallingly uneven paving slab, and through no fault of her own, the car bumped over a ridge and clipped a lamp-post, which subsequently toppled over, blocking the road for five-and-a-half hours.'

'The paper said there were no other vehicles involved.'

'A conspiracy, apparently, though I'm not quite sure what or who it's against.'

'Is she still talking about getting compensation from the instructor?' Poppy asked.

'Yeah, and something about the European Court of Human Rights.'

Poppy laughed and then stopped herself, feeling bad for making fun of her friend behind her back, even though it had been like this forever. When Mark wasn't around, she and Freya would gossip about him; when Freya was somewhere else, Poppy and Mark would talk about her. It dawned on Poppy, for the first time, that this likely meant Mark and Freya chatted about her when they were alone.

The crash *was* funny, though – especially the front-page picture of it on the Ledford *Ledger*, the local newspaper of the neighbouring town. It showed the learner car embedded in a hedge, its airbags hanging limply, with a lamp-post lying at a right angle to where it should have been. Freya hadn't been hurt, although she did occasionally clutch the back of her neck when she remembered that she'd told them she had whiplash.

Mark calmed himself, likely realising it was a bit mean to talk about his girlfriend in such a way when she wasn't there. 'What did Frey get you for your birthday?' he asked, changing the subject.

'A top that was too big. I think it might've been something she was given that was too small for her.'

'Sounds about right. What did you get from anyone else?'

'Odds and ends. Bits and bobs. Not much. Everyone goes big for sixteen or eighteen. You get stitched up at seventeen.'

Mark crouched and reached into his satchel, removing a rectangular package that was wrapped in bright paper patterned with pictures of dogs. 'Ta-da!' he said as he held it out for Poppy to take.

It was thin, solid and surprisingly heavy considering it wasn't that big. Poppy rotated it in her hand, looking at the different dog breeds on the paper.

'I could've just got you a roll of paper if that's all you're interested in,' Mark said.

'I'm taking my time.'

'Bor-ing! Open it.'

Poppy tugged at the tightly wrapped ribbon, but not hard enough to break it. There was a red bow stuck to the centre.

'There's no way you wrapped this yourself,' she said.

'Who says?'

'I do. Boys can't wrap.'

'What about Eminem?'

'You're not funny.'

Mark thumped his chest. 'I man. I do anything.'

'Who wrapped it?'

His shoulders slumped, though his smile remained. 'Mum. I bought it, though – and the paper. I did *try* to wrap it but, well… Too much paper and way too much tape. I ended up sticking my thumbs together. Dad was laughing so much, he spilled his tea on the carpet.' He gave Poppy a double thumbs-up, which had her giggling again.

'You gonna open it, then?' he asked.

'But it's wrapped so neatly.'

'Open it!'

Poppy did as she was told, jabbing a fingernail into the square edges and ripping the paper away. It only took her a few seconds to figure out what he'd given her. At first she was confused, but he caught her eye as she looked up.

'It's the exact same set of pencils as last year,' he said. 'I'm going to give you the same present every year to make sure you don't stop drawing.'

Poppy ran her fingers across the cool metal of the tin before putting it to one side. She stood and crossed the room without a word, bending down to hug Mark where he sat in the armchair. It should have been awkward but her chin slotted perfectly into the crook of his neck and shoulder. He pressed his hands into her back. Poppy closed her eyes and breathed in. She wasn't sure what his hair smelled of. It certainly wasn't the half-tub of gel that some of the lads used – the ones who turned up to college looking like they'd drowned. It was nicer than that. Comforting. Mark's fingers tightened, and she could feel him clasping her into him. She knew she should pull away, but they felt like a pair of puzzle pieces that fitted perfectly, so she didn't.

'Thank you,' she whispered.

'For the pencils?'

He sounded confused, like this was too much of a gesture for something so simple. It wasn't the gift itself for which she was grateful, it was the way he knew her. Twelve months before, when he'd bought her the pencils for the first time, Poppy had used them because it would have seemed wasteful not to. Without them, she might not have bothered to continue drawing. She definitely wouldn't have switched from A-level History to A-level Art. Before Mark's gift, drawing had only ever been something Poppy had liked – a doodle or two in her free time. It wasn't something she'd taken seriously. But over the year, she'd worn those pencils down to pointed stubs. Mark had seen that, so had got her the exact same gift.

Mark patted Poppy's back gently and she pulled away. Their faces were at the same level.

Their eyes.

Their noses.

Their mouths.

Their lips.

For a second, they stared at each other, neither daring to speak. Two seconds. Three. Poppy could feel his warm breath on her face.

Then he blinked.

'I should probably go,' Mark said softly.

Poppy stepped backwards, nodding too quickly. 'Right, er… I have stuff to do anyway.'

He stood hurriedly, turning and not looking back as he rushed through the house towards the front door. She heard him mutter a 'see ya' as he opened it, and then he was gone, off into the summer heat to catch the bus and meet his girlfriend.

Poppy's best friend.

His departure happened so quickly that Poppy was left standing in her living room, watching through the front window as Mark almost ran from the house.

She didn't blame him.

It had only been a few seconds, a momentary blip considering how long they'd known each other, and yet… Poppy didn't know what she would have done had Mark not blinked.

My dearest Poppy,

Happy birthday.

Seventeen is a strange age. When you turn sixteen, there are plenty of things you're legally allowed to do, even more at eighteen (the fun stuff comes then!). But at seventeen, not so much changes.

Obviously you are now allowed to learn to drive but, after a bit of digging around, I found out you can also apply for a pilot's licence. Just note that, as your mother, I expressly forbid you from crashing planes. Actually, as a general rule, I'd prefer it if you could go through your life without crashing anything, except for perhaps a pedalo or dodgems – something like that.

Assuming you haven't spent the day taking flying lessons – and even if you have – I hope this letter finds you well.

I want to tell you something I've never told you before.

When I was seventeen, I was obsessed with a boy. Actually, I was obsessed with him when I was sixteen and fifteen as well. Perhaps at fourteen, too. Let's just say that, for a significant part of my early to mid-teens, I was infatuated with a boy.

His name was Jacob and I used to scrawl his name all over my various school workbooks and the like. I only hope those books have long since been burned because, if they still exist, the embarrassment would be my one reason to be grateful for my current state.

You know that sport has never been my thing, but Jacob played cricket. Because of that, I would go to Ledford Cricket Club every Saturday. My friend Sharon and I would take books and a picnic basket, then we'd camp on the edge of the field and spend the next six hours trying to pretend we had a clue what was going on.

If that wasn't bad enough, Jacob's brother worked in a garage near the school during the week. Every lunchtime, Sharon and I would go and sit in this café across the road. The food was awful, either undercooked or overcooked but never well-cooked. We'd order whatever we could afford and sit in the window, hoping Jacob would walk past on his way to visit his brother. I have no idea what I thought might happen if he did. At best, I'd have waved, he'd have waved back – and that would have been that. At worst, he wouldn't even have known who I was.

He noticed me eventually, though – and when I hadn't even been trying. It wasn't at cricket or in that café; it was in the park. I was on my way home, carrying three bags of shopping, when the laws of physics decided that a) the weight of the shopping was heavier than b) the strength of the bag, meaning that c) everything spilled onto the floor.

Don't quote me on any of that if you've ended up studying physics.

Anyway, the result was catastrophic. There were apples rolling down the hill, lemonade bottles foaming so much that the lids popped off and created fizzy fountains of sugar, a smashed jar of raspberry jam that instantly attracted a swarm of ants – and so on.

As I chased after the apples, Jacob was coming the other way. I was so panicky that I didn't even recognise him when he picked up a shattered packet of digestive biscuits and helped me repair the bag. By the time I'd come to my senses, he'd said something like, 'Aren't you that girl from the cricket?' Usually, I'd have gone a bit giggly and made a fool of myself, but on that occasion, I somehow managed to tell him my name and that was that.

Jacob was my first proper boyfriend and, my word, was I happy with myself. I continued to follow him everywhere, except that I now had a legitimate reason to.

There was a problem, though. Throughout the years I'd been etching Jacob's name onto my workbooks, I'd also been creating this perfect figure in my mind. Not only did he have the slightly curly blond hair and lovely eyebrows (don't ask), he was also funny and caring, not to mention interested in all the same things that I was.

Except that he wasn't.

Because he never had been.

He liked cricket, football and cars, and he didn't want to come to the cinema with Sharon and me to watch Disney movies. He didn't want to go shopping on a weekend, or spend hours sitting on the wall outside of Debenhams, listening to the radio and talking about bands.

We went out for about a month and then it ended. He broke up with me and I cried for about three days. Shortly after that, he started seeing this girl named Erin and I was devastated all over again.

It all seems so silly now, but I'm kind of pleased it's a part of me.

Of course, time passed and I met your father. He wasn't, nor would he ever be, second best, but he certainly wasn't who I had dreamed of marrying back when I was seventeen! My point is that there are times in life when things don't go your way. It might be a job that you really want, something you want to buy but can't afford, a gig you want to attend but can't – and so on. Big disappointments, small disappointments. A boy you want to be with, but can't…

What's important isn't the setback, it's what you do afterwards.

That doesn't mean 'everything happens for a reason', because it doesn't. People who say that are kidding themselves, trying to pretend that there are no negatives in life, that everything's a good thing. It's really not.

Setbacks and disappointments might make you a stronger person because you deal with them and then carry on. But sometimes we have to accept that they happen with no rhyme or reason. It's too easy to obsess about things over which we have no control. If there's one thing I hope you take from this, it's that there's no point in doing that. Tomorrow's another day, after all.

If not that, then make sure you use proper carrier bags at the supermarket.

I love you,

Mum

Poppy was sitting on her bed when her father knocked gently on the door. Déjà vu of twelve months previously. It was past ten at night. She called for him to enter. His dark hair was damp, clinging to the top of his ears, and his suit was unbuttoned and darker than usual.

'Is it raining out?' Poppy asked.

He shook his head. 'Next door's sprinklers went off as I was walking past. Bloody things have a life of their own.'

Poppy giggled. 'That's your excuse and you're sticking to it?' she said.

'That's my excuse.'

He sat on the end of her bed, making it sink slightly. He clutched the base of his back. 'Happy birthday, Pops. Sorry I had to go so early. Did you have a good day?'

Poppy sat up a little, cradling her knees to her chest. She was in her favourite pyjamas, the fleecy green ones patterned by bears. They might be old, they might be childish, and it was probably too warm for them – but, *sometimes*, fleecy green pyjamas with bears on were what she needed.

'It was OK.'

For a moment, her father said nothing, his mouth open a little, tongue pressed to the top of his mouth. 'I know I'm not entirely up with teenager speak nowadays – but is that "OK", as in "best day ever", or "OK", as in "not so good"?'

Poppy glanced over his shoulder, avoiding his smile, not wanting it to spread. 'Just OK.'

She picked her mother's letter up from the nightstand and passed it across. Her dad took it and stared at the handwriting on the front of the envelope. He ran his thumb across Poppy's name but didn't open it. 'This is between you and your mum,' he said, putting it down on the bed.

'I'm not sure if I want to read the others. It's not that I don't love her, it's just…' Poppy's voice cracked but she forced herself to finish. 'It's just that I miss her.'

She gulped away the lump in her throat, but it returned in an instant. Her dad leaned forward, placing a slightly wet hand on her shoulder. She didn't mind, pulling herself closer to him, feeling the dampness of his suit.

'I miss her too, Pops,' he said.

Eighteen

Poppy crouched, resting her elbow on the table and scrubbing the cloth across the surface as vigorously as she could. If there was one thing recent times had taught her, it was that coffee stains were the absolute worst. Well, bloodstains *might* be worse but she hadn't yet had the misfortune of having to clear up someone's blood.

There was still time…

After half-a-dozen violent swipes, the brown ring finally dissolved from the table, so Poppy set about clearing up the rest of the crap that had been left. The leather sofa and floor was littered with balled-up tissues, enough cookie crumbs to start a biscuit beach, four plastic stirrers and some dust-covered raisins – which was particularly annoying, as Cipriani's Coffee Shop didn't even sell dried fruit.

Poppy brushed everything into a dustpan and then weaved around a child in a high chair who was lashing out at thin air with his feet. A future Premier League footballer in training. He belonged to one of the yummy mummies who had parked a tank of a 4x4 on the road outside. She was a familiar face who came to the café every couple of days to drink skinny lattes with her fellow new-mum friends. Their little darlings were allowed to bite, hit and kick anyone in the near vicinity because any sort of discipline might impinge upon their children's creative freedom. Poppy didn't have much time for the yummy mummy brigade. They were bad tippers, too.

She dumped the rubbish into the bin and leaned against the counter, stretching tall and feeling her back crick with almost overwhelming satisfaction.

'Poooooooppy!'

Poppy broke from her moment of rest, spinning at the sound of what was almost her name.

'What?' she replied, barely managing to keep the annoyance from her voice.

Mr Cipriani had his hands on his hips, one foot metronoming on the floor as he nodded towards the couple standing on the other side of the counter. Poppy didn't know exactly how old Mr Cipriani was, but his browny-orange skin was wrinkled like a cheap leather handbag off the market. His age hadn't stopped his hair from growing, though, with manic white threads sprouting from his scalp like the seeds of a dandelion. Hair nets for food preparation definitely weren't his thing.

'Customers,' he snapped, in his thick Mediterranean accent.

'I was only—'

'Customers!'

Poppy's boss turned and shuffled back into the kitchen without another word. She gave his back her absolute best glare, the one she saved for when her dad wouldn't let her stay out, or for when he started going on about her paying rent again.

A blink later and she was back to happy, smiley, please-leave-me-a-tip Poppy. She took the couple's order while absent-mindedly asking how their day had been, not bothering to listen to the answer. Most people gave the usual, 'good, thanks' anyway. Like a reflex.

'How's your day going?'

'Good, thanks.'

Only the maniacs went into more detail than that, listing hospital appointments and various illnesses, or banging on about the traffic.

As the couple went to sit on the newly cleared table, Poppy started packing coffee granules into the filter basket. She jumped as a hand tapped her shoulder, and turned to see a grinning mound of dreadlocks.

'Need a hand?' the owner of the dreadlocks asked.

Poppy made a point of rolling her eyes. 'Your breaks are getting longer.'

Clyde looked over her shoulder to the clock above the espresso machine. 'It's only five past one.' He flashed a toothy, lopsided smile. His teeth were so white that Poppy often wondered if he'd had something done to them. He was a few years older than her, with dark skin so perfectly smooth that he could easily pass for younger. Poppy wanted to be annoyed with him, but it was so difficult to be irritated with Clyde. His smile was infectious, a weapon that he used dozens of times a day. Poppy doubted he'd ever been in trouble. Not *real* trouble, anyway.

Without further conversation, Clyde started to fill the couple's order, clinking and clanking his way around the coffee machine and finally giving Poppy a moment of respite.

'You 'K?' he asked, over his shoulder.

Poppy loosened her apron and wiped her brow. It was steaming outside and not much better in the café. She fought back a yawn: 'Just tired – and hot.'

'This is cold for Mr C.'

'He's been on me all morning again, even when I only stop for a second.'

Clyde shrugged, not wanting to take sides. He never did. If people were countries, he'd be Switzerland: sitting in the middle and never committing to a point of view – even if one – Mr Cipriani – was a potential Nazi. Poppy turned back to the till, knowing there was no point in complaining to him.

With no one else to serve, she emptied the tip jar onto the counter. She pushed anything smaller than ten pence back into the glass jar, hoping it would make some of the future customers feel guilty, and then counted what was left.

After a manic morning's work, she and Clyde had barely eight pounds between them. Eight sodding pounds. Her feet were sore, her eyelids heavy, her shoulders ached, her was hair damp with sweat, her ears had been half-chewed off by Mr Cipriani and, for all that, she was on minimum wage – plus four extra quid.

'Right,' a familiar voice bellowed. 'I want a large cappuccino, four sugars, a double chocolate mocha muffin and one of those little caramel biscuit things that you get on the side.'

Poppy looked up from the counter to see Freya standing on the other side. She was wearing a strappy purple top, denim hot pants and tights, blue canvas trainers and an enormous grin. Her hair had gone frizzy in the heat and she was bouncing with energy.

'What are you doing in Ledford?' Poppy asked.

Freya pointed a thumb over her shoulder towards a sheepish-looking Mark. '*We're* your birthday presents.' She flung her arms wide. 'Surpriiiiise!'

Clyde was suddenly at Poppy's side. 'It's your birthday?'

'Her eighteenth,' Freya declared, before Poppy could say anything.

Clyde nudged Poppy's shoulder with his elbow. He was at least eight inches taller than her. 'Why didn't you say something?' he asked.

'It never came up,' Poppy replied quickly, wanting to get out of the conversation. She caught Mark's eye and, without needing to say anything, she knew that he knew.

'Is it your lunch break yet?' Mark asked.

'I, er…'

'Go,' Clyde said. 'I'll cover.' He nodded at Freya and repeated her order back, before taking Mark's and telling Poppy he'd bring her something over.

Freya skipped out of the café and plopped onto one of the metal chairs on the pavement. She shunted it out from under the parasol into the sun with an ear-crunching screech and then took her phone out of her bag. She tapped at the screen, not looking up.

'Getting to Ledford is *way* easier now we don't have to take the bus, Pops.'

Poppy turned to Mark, who was scratching his chin. 'You drove?'

'I thought… *We* thought it'd be nice to come and say happy birthday. I'm working tonight, so wouldn't have seen you otherwise.'

Freya returned her phone to her bag, removing three university prospectuses and dropping them on the table. The top one sported a cover with three laughing young people walking across an emerald lawn, bright blue sky above, sun beaming down. 'PLYMOUTH' was emblazoned across the front, as if to point out that the only weather the south-west ever got was sent straight from heaven.

'Does this mean you've settled on Plymouth if you get the grades?' Poppy asked.

Freya started to flick through the pages, nodding. '*If*…'

'You'll be fine,' Mark said.

He'd clearly meant this to be supportive but Freya was rarely far from one of her moods. She flashed a finger towards him. 'Just because *you're* guaranteed straight A's.'

'I'm not.'

Freya flicked her hair and huffed something under her breath. Tension between her and Mark had been building ever since they'd taken their A levels a few weeks previously. The results were due in a fortnight. For Freya, they would decide which university she ended up attending. Mark's destination was already settled. He was right, he wasn't *guaranteed* straight A's – but they all knew he'd do well.

'How was your trip to Manchester?' Poppy asked, ignoring Freya's second huff.

'All right,' Mark replied. 'I've got a provisional place in halls, assuming my results come through. It's in a nice area and it looks like there's loads going on. I had a chat with someone from the students' union and there are all sorts of clubs.'

Freya muttered something else inaudible.

Poppy risked a quick peek into the café. Mr Cipriani was standing at the counter, having one of his laughing, matey conversations with Clyde. He might be harsh with Poppy but he treated Clyde like the son he didn't have. He also clearly had eyes in the back of his head because, as Poppy watched, his face spun towards her like a ventriloquist's puppet. His gaze locked with hers before he glanced down at his watch. Poppy turned back to the table, trying to ignore him.

'When did you start doing that?' Mark asked.

'Huh?'

He nodded down to the napkin underneath her hand. Without thinking about it, Poppy had been doodling with the pen she used to take down orders. She looked down. It was only a series of swirls and swishes, nothing special.

Poppy shrugged. 'I dunno.'

She screwed up the napkin and pushed it into the pocket at the front of her apron before he could examine it any more closely.

Freya slapped the Plymouth prospectus closed and dropped it into her bag. She started biting her nails, bored. 'Whatcha gonna do, Pops?'

'About what?'

She nodded at the café. 'This. You gonna try college again next year? It's not like they kicked you out, just said you'd have to sort out your grades. You could— Ow!' She flung her arms up and scowled at Mark. 'Whatcha kick me for?'

'It was an, er… accident.'

They stared at each other for a moment. Poppy guessed they'd spent large parts of the drive to the café talking about her.

'I'm not going back,' Poppy said, regaining their attention. 'I dropped out because I didn't want to be at college any more. I'm fine doing this.'

She spoke firmly but knew it wasn't true. Not entirely, anyway. She hadn't completely given up on education but couldn't take being at college every day. She couldn't be the two-plus-one any longer.

That was the real reason she'd dropped out. As for being 'fine' working at the café…

She was saved from having to expand on this because Clyde appeared at the table, holding a tray aloft. He gave Freya her cappuccino and muffin, as well as two biscuits and half-a-dozen packets of sugar. Freya yelped with glee and started emptying sugar into her drink as Clyde placed the rest of the order on the table. Poppy ended up with a strawberry lemonade that was at least sixty per cent ice, plus a key lime cupcake with a single candle poking out of the top.

'You ready?' Clyde asked.

'For what?' Poppy replied.

Clyde delved into his pocket and pulled out a lighter. In one swift movement, the wick was lit and he started singing an almost in-tune

'Happy Birthday'. Poppy shrank into her chair, pretending to be embarrassed. Mark was mouthing the words but Poppy didn't think he was actually singing. Freya, however, was giving it the full Sunday morning gospel choir rendition – minus the correct pitch, key or tune.

When the song finished, the three of them applauded themselves and then Clyde told Poppy to make a wish.

Poppy eyed the flickering flame atop the cake and then closed her eyes to give the impression she was thinking of something. She had made all her wishes three years ago and none of them had come true, so why would today be any different?

'Whatcha wish for?' Freya asked, as Poppy opened her eyes.

Poppy blew out the candle but didn't reply, accidentally catching Mark's gaze as she looked up. He was smiling with his lips but not with his eyes. If anything, he looked apologetic. Poppy had not seen much of him so far this summer, partly because of her job and partly because of his studies. He'd been helping out on one of his uncle's farms, too, leaving his face and arms golden brown. His naturally dark hair had been lightened by the sun. His thicker beard made him look more of a man than ever before.

'If she tells you her wish, it won't come true,' Mark said.

'Ah, that's rubbish,' Freya replied. 'We're friends.'

Clyde had taken a step backwards from the table, ready to return inside, but Freya flashed a hand towards him. 'Hey, Clyde. You comin' out tonight?'

'Er…'

'You've gotta come out. It's Pops' birthday.'

For once, Clyde seemed off-guard, glancing quickly inside and then back again. He was avoiding looking at Poppy, too. 'Where are you going?'

'You know the Kicking Horse down the road? There, for nine o'clock. Pops is old enough to drink legally now.'

'I suppose, I'm, er...'

Freya clicked her fingers. 'Woo! That's settled then. We are getting battered tonight.'

Clyde nodded and returned into the café, leaving the three of them alone.

'Why'd you invite him?' Poppy hissed.

'Cos he is properly gorgeous, Pops – and he's *always* looking at you. Ooh, I'd love to tug on those dreads.' Freya nudged Mark with her elbow. 'Don't worry though, babes, I only have eyes for you.'

Mark seemed anything but worried. He was staring, unfocused, past Poppy towards the end of the street.

Poppy said very little during the rest of her break. Freya listed the drinks she was planning to get through that evening. Poppy had two bites of her cake and let Freya have the rest, then caught herself doodling again. She screwed up the napkin before Mark could say anything.

It wasn't long before Mr Cipriani found his way onto the pavement. He said nothing directly to Poppy but strode slowly up and down along the tables and chairs. It did nothing to dispel Poppy's notion that he might be some sort of Nazi. She took the hint, finished her glass of melted ice, said goodbye to her friends, and headed back to work.

My dearest Poppy,

I know we had a few conversations about what you might or might not do when school finishes. I didn't stay in education past the age of sixteen. Times are different now, so it might be hard for you to understand this, but I never even considered it.

What did happen when I left school was that my mother said that as long as I was living at home, I had to contribute to the household in some way. What she really wanted was for me to settle down with a man – preferably one of the local farmer's lads with a bit of money and land – and start having babies. She'd married my father when she was still in her teens, had me a year later, and then watched him go off to serve in the army shortly after that. Of course, I didn't know any of this until much later. Settling down young and having a family was what she thought a young woman ought to want from the world.

By the time I'd turned eighteen, I hadn't found a man to settle down with but I couldn't face living at home any longer, either. My mother and I didn't exactly row but we didn't get on. I decided that if she wanted me to 'contribute', then I'd be better off spending that money on a place of my own.

I ended up living in a tiny bedsit in Ledford. It was only one room. The living-room sofa folded out to create a bed, and the kitchen existed in the same space. It was a far cry from my mother's four-bedroom house. The entire bedsit was about the same size as my bedroom at home. At first, I wasn't sure I could cope – and yet I couldn't go back, because I'd told my mother I was leaving. No big huff, more a declaration of intent. Not as dramatic as when you told me you would not eat sprouts, regardless of it being Christmas. With me, there was a lot less stamping of feet and I didn't throw anything. (Yes, I do remember!)

Back then, there was no such thing as a minimum wage. I worked in a bakery in Ledford for an absolute pittance. This was before supermarkets and chains took over. The bakery's not there any longer. It was a small independent place that had been in the town for years by the time I worked there. It was run by a man named Baker.

Yes, really!

There was a Mr Butcher next door, with a Mr Candlestick-maker on the other side.

Actually, there wasn't, but the name did make me smile. I often wondered if Mr Baker had ever considered a different career, or if he felt destined because of the name. If so, I pity the poor child born to Mr Toilet Cleaner!

Anyway, it was my job to get in early and start the ovens warming. After that, I'd set to work on making the dough before Mr Baker got in and started to knead. That was always his job because, in his words, 'your hands are too small'. I'd deal with the customers at the front of the shop while he wrestled the dough at the back. The work wasn't that hard but it was a lot of early mornings and long hours for not a lot of money. It did mean I could afford the rent on that bedsit, though, which was my main concern.

We had a lot of repeat customers: locals who came by to order the same type of bread every couple of days. For example, I remember there was this man named Mr Peters who always came in at exactly 7.33 each morning. It got to the point where I stopped checking the clock over the shop door when he appeared, because I already knew what time it was. He was tall and wore a suit with shiny shoes. He always carried a newspaper under his arm. He'd say hello to me and had somehow learned my first name, although I didn't remember telling it to him. He'd then buy a Cornish pasty and be on his way. He did that every day for months. I used to joke with him, asking if he wanted to try something different, but he'd smile, say he was fine, then head off with his pasty. I still have such a clear memory of him that it's like I saw him only this morning.

Then there was this young boy who always came in with his mother. They were never separate, and never with anyone else – always just her and him. She used to wear a blue padded body warmer all the time, even when it was sunny. Her son was this really tiny thing: so skinny that you could see the angles of his bones through his clothes. He looked permanently dirty, with these brown crusts of soil or food around his chin. He always wore the same clothes, too: brown flared trousers with a jumper that was too big for him. He never said anything.

The mother would buy a full loaf of bread every other day. One time, they were in the bakery together and the boy was standing a bit behind his mother – as always. It was coming up to Easter, which was a busy time. Most shops used to close for the whole of the weekend, so people stocked up ahead of Good Friday.

The woman wanted her bread as usual but we'd had a bad batch of yeast and some loaves hadn't risen. Mr Baker was busy taking a new batch out of the oven, so there was going to be a five-minute wait. The woman was fine with that. She pottered around, writing in this little notebook she had. No smartphones for note-taking then! I have no idea what she was writing.

Soon after, Mr Baker came out from the back with the fresh loaves. He was all smiles and apologies and everything was fine. Then he noticed our display of Easter biscuits in the window. There had been a stack of perhaps a dozen or so, but there were now only four. He asked me when we'd sold the others and I replied that we hadn't.

It's really hard to describe what happened next. It felt like time slowed down. There was this moment where Mr Baker, the mother and I all turned to look at the son. He was sitting close to the window, legs crossed, looking as guilty as anyone's ever looked. And I knew he'd stolen them. They'd be in his pockets or his bag, perhaps both. But I also knew this kid was starving. He was so thin that he looked ill. Mr Baker was about to go around the counter to confront him and I had this moment of clarity, as if I already knew everything that was about to happen.

Before anyone could say anything else, I said, 'I ate them.' I blurted it out and the three of them all turned to look at me. The kid's eyes were enormous, like massive saucers. Mr Baker asked me to repeat myself, so I did.

The kid and his mum left and it was just me and Mr Baker. I remember he had this really sad look on his face, as if he'd been standing next to the oven for too long and his skin had melted. Everything about him had sagged. I had a lump in my throat because I knew what was coming. He was staring off towards the front door, unable to look at me properly. He said that he couldn't abide dishonesty. That eating those biscuits was thieving. That if I'd asked, it would have been fine. Because I hadn't, I'd crossed a line.

He said sorry three or four times – and then he sacked me. He said he would pay me until the end of the week but that was the end of it.

I'm not entirely sure what I did for the rest of that day but I do remember the evening. I was in my bedsit with my friend Sharon, crying like a newborn. It wasn't the job so much, more that I didn't know what I'd do next. I didn't want to go back to my mum's house, because I'd get the 'I told-you-so' look. I couldn't believe what I'd done. I'd taken the blame for some kid whose name I didn't even know. When Sharon asked what happened, I found

I couldn't tell her the true story. I didn't think she'd understand. I told her that I ate some biscuits and Mr Baker sacked me. The lie became the truth because the truth was too strange.

My rent was due a week later, so I only had a few days in which to try to find a new job. I spent the whole of the next day searching for work. Bear in mind I had few qualifications, no experience, and no references. I went to the job centre but they had nothing for me. I went into Ledford's shops to ask if they needed anyone; I checked out all the noticeboards, but I couldn't find anything.

That evening, I went back to my bedsit dejected. It was the day before Good Friday. Everything was going to be shut for the weekend and I had no idea what I was going to do. I was thinking about getting a bus back to Purley – to Mum's house – when there was a knock at my door. At that time, it was only really Sharon who knew where I lived, so I assumed it was her. I opened up and it was Mr Peters.

He was still wearing his suit, with the newspaper under his arm. I suppose I must have been open-mouthed, because he started to explain himself really quickly. He said he'd been to the bakery that morning and of course he'd not seen me. He'd asked after me, and Mr Baker had told him I no longer worked there. He'd sensed there was more to the story and knew where I lived because he'd seen me locking my front door one weekend. He had come to ask what had happened.

It was really odd to have him turn up at my door. I'm not sure I can explain why he did, other than because of those one-minute snippets of conversation. We'd spoken every day for months and it felt like we knew each other to a certain degree. He seemed like a nice man.

I ended up telling him that I'd eaten some biscuits without asking, some stupid Easter biscuits, and that I'd been deservedly sacked.

He stared at me and it was as if he knew I was lying. He bit his lip and I couldn't meet his eyes because the lump in my throat was there again. It felt like I might cry. It sounds so strange to say this now – it was strange then, really – but there was this moment where it felt like he'd read my thoughts. That he knew exactly what had happened and why I'd taken the blame.

He told me that his firm had a job opening and he was wondering if I'd be interested. He said he'd met people with qualifications as long as his arm but he wanted someone who knew how to smile and really mean it. He gave me a card and said that he'd see me on Tuesday if I was interested.

What happened then is a story for another time.

But what I learned was that, sometimes, short-term things have long-term consequences. On the surface, that bakery job was turning on the oven and taking people's money. Beyond that, it was so much more. It was a small, low-paid job I did to pay the rent but I ended up meeting someone who changed my life.

Today you turn eighteen years old. This will be a time in your life where you'll be thinking about the future, about where life will take you. Your friends, your father and – more than anyone – your own self, will be putting pressure on you to make decisions about courses, jobs and everything else. People will want you to grow up quickly, but here's the truth:

It's OK not to have all the answers right now.

It really is.

The craziest thing about forcing young people to make lasting decisions about the rest of their life is that there's an assumption that they won't change. The opposite is true. If you're the same person with the same interests at thirty as you were at eighteen, then something's gone badly wrong.

Of course, if possible, you should aim for a job or career within a field you love, but there's enjoyment to be had in many places. That might mean using a job as a means to an end. Like turning on the ovens in a bakery, for instance. An occupation might not be much fun in itself but if it allows you money, friends, contacts, ideas and experience, then there's every chance you can use those to enhance your life further along the line.

The power of the young is so apparent now. You see it in TV talent shows; you see it in sport. There are wonderfully gifted teenagers who are famous and rich beyond most people's wildest dreams. The other side of that is that so many young people see their successful peers and think that if they've not made it by twenty-one or so, they're a failure.

That couldn't be further from the truth.

If you're lucky, life lasts a long time – and it's the long game that counts. Be happy – and happy birthday.

Mum

Poppy was sitting on the sofa in her living room, flicking through the messages on her phone while keeping one eye on the clock at the top of the screen. She looked up as her dad entered the room, his sleeves rolled up, flecks of washing-up suds soaking into the hairs on his hands.

'What time are you going out?' he asked, even though he'd asked the exact same question an hour previously.

Poppy didn't look up. 'Fifteen minutes ago, supposedly. Mark's driving to Ledford. We're getting a taxi back, then he's going to catch the bus to pick up his car tomorrow.'

She knew what he was really asking: had she planned a safe journey out and back? Poppy thought about listing the other ways she was going to behave responsibly – such as returning at a certain time – but she didn't want to make any promises. The last thing she wanted was her dad calling at midnight to make sure she was all right.

Her father sat in the armchair, eyes flicking past the envelope that Poppy had left on the window sill. Her name was on the front, facing out. She wanted her dad to ask about it, perhaps even for him to read it when she'd left the house. However, he didn't mention it and neither did she.

'Are you sure you're not hungry?' he asked.

'I've eaten, Dad.'

He stared at her as if he didn't believe it, though he didn't press. 'And are you sure you liked your present?'

Poppy fingered the necklace she was wearing. Unlike Freya, she wasn't one for jewellery, yet her father had found something that was neither overly chunky, nor understated to the point of being futile. It had pretty leaf shapes fitted into the chain and, though white gold, didn't feel too heavy. He'd told her he wanted to give her something permanent for her eighteenth, a keepsake. Although she would have preferred money, it was hard to argue with.

'It's fine,' Poppy replied – too harshly, she knew.

Her father pressed back in his seat, chastened by her tone, but not wanting an argument. At least he hadn't brought up paying rent again. He was probably trying to teach her the value of money but, well – he could knob off.

Poppy knew she should apologise, but so far, nothing about her birthday had gone the way she'd wanted. After a long, hot day at work, she was ready for a proper – one hundred per cent legal – night on the lash.

Her phone's clock blinked forward by another minute. Sixteen minutes late now. Mark might be driving but the delay would undoubtedly be down to Freya.

Sixty more awkward seconds.

She could feel her dad wanting to say something, mouth bobbing open awkwardly like a fish's and then closing again.

Seventeen minutes late.

Finally, the doorbell rang. Poppy leapt up before her father could move, muttering a quick, 'See ya,' and then rushing into the hallway.

The 'big night' Freya had promised wasn't materialising, with Poppy's birthday not much improving from the disaster it had already been. Poppy had left the organising to Freya but should have known better. Instead of the riotous house party that had been Freya's own eighteenth, the Kicking Horse pub was providing an atmosphere that managed to be both overbearing and underwhelmingly dull.

The music was so loud that conversations had to be conducted through a mix of shouting and lip-reading, yet the place was largely deserted, save for a few middle-aged women who should have known better. The bar was covered with glittering lights and stacks of upturned sparkling glasses, while the DJ loved the sound of his own voice.

As if there was a DJ who didn't.

It was the type of flashy, empty place that Freya loved. The only thing saving the night from total catastrophe was the two-for-one cocktails – plus Freya, Mark and Clyde keeping Poppy in drinks.

There wasn't anyone else out with them. Most of Poppy's college friends had evaporated when she'd left. Plenty had already disappeared off for a gap year now that the exams were over. Not that they were her *real* friends – more people who she knew. Whether she liked it or not, Poppy's only *real* friends were those currently sitting with her around the table.

Poppy downed her third tequila… something. It was an orangey-red and tasted sweeter than her birthday cake. Good job she wasn't still counting carbs. Just as she was beginning to think the night wouldn't get any better, the music volume mercifully dimmed. It took her a few moments to clock this because of the residual ringing in her ears, but then suddenly she could hear Freya.

'… looks really expensive.'

'Huh?' Poppy replied.

Freya nodded at Poppy. 'The necklace your dad got you. Must've cost a fortune?'

Poppy found herself touching it defensively. The metal was clammy with her sweat. Freya was wearing a shop-full of jewellery herself – three different necklaces, each progressively chunkier, a variety of hoops on her wrists, and big dangly earrings. It had always been her way.

Poppy shrugged. 'I guess.'

'You're so lucky.'

'Why?'

'My mum got me a bus pass for my birthday. A *bus* pass!'

Mark leaned in. 'You've used it loads – and she got you other stuff, too.'

'Why're you defending her?'

'I'm not, but—'

Freya grabbed his hand and pulled him to his feet. She glanced between Poppy and Clyde with a wicked grin. 'Shut up, come dance with me.'

Mark was yanked away from the table, not exactly fighting his girlfriend but dragging his feet nonetheless. He watched Poppy over his shoulder until Freya pulled him past the pillar that was mystifyingly in the centre of the dance floor. Moments later, Freya's arms were around Mark's neck and they were swallowed by the shadows close to the toilets.

Who said romance was dead?

Clyde had been taking it easy, refusing spirits and drinking only half-pints of cider. He was cradling a glass close to his lips when he leaned in towards Poppy, giving her his full toothy grin. 'She could've made that a bit more obvious.'

It took Poppy a second to realise what he meant. 'I, er… Yeah.' She tried to think of something funny to say in reply, but came up with nothing. She couldn't remember ever having had a conversation with Clyde about something other than work. 'It's supposed to be sunny again tomorrow,' she said, eventually.

He bit his lip, nodding. 'So they say.'

The music volume increased a little but not enough to stifle conversation completely. Which was a shame.

Poppy sipped at her fourth Tequila Something, wishing it was stronger. There was a tingling beginning around her temples but she was hoping to blast through tipsiness into full-on drunkenness. She hid behind the cocktail glass as she tried to think of something to say. What did people normally talk about? She couldn't go on about college – and anyway, she'd prefer to forget that chapter of her life. She still lived with her dad, didn't own a car and didn't do much away from work except hang around with Freya and Mark. With the pair of them nicking off to university in a month or so, she wouldn't even have that to talk about any more.

'Vodafone are rubbish, aren't they?' she said, holding up her phone.

'I'm not with them,' Clyde replied, which shut down that particular topic. Poppy tried to remember anything he might be interested in. Music? He definitely sang to himself around the café and she was pretty sure he had a guitar. But what type of music would he be into? She didn't want to bang on about some band she thought were great, only for him to say they were terrible.

Poppy took a bigger mouthful of her drink.

This would be a lot easier if she was pissed. Why was Clyde even here? It was her birthday, her *eighteenth* birthday, and here she was with a lad she'd not even invited.

She offered Clyde a weak smile as he tossed a dreadlock over his shoulder. He seemed happy enough, as if hanging around in pubs not saying much was normal for him. Perhaps it was?

'You'll never guess what I heard about Mr C,' he said, leaning in conspiratorially.

'What?'

'Y'know he's always away on weekends?'

'Yeah…'

'I know this lad who used to work at the café before us. He moved up to Cardiff and reckons he's seen Mr C out and about on the weekends.'

'Oh, right…' This was not much of a revelation. Poppy had thought it would be better than that.

Clyde was unperturbed by her lack of reaction, leaning in even closer, yet somehow slouching at the same time. 'He's not just out, he's *out*. He goes cross-dressing: short skirt, make-up, the lot.'

His white teeth shone in the bluey-purple light overhead as he raised an eyebrow and started to laugh. Poppy tried to imagine Mr Cipriani – with his olive skin, deep-set wrinkles and permanent chef's apron – wearing a dress. He'd have hairy legs and his wild, white hair would make him look even more ridiculous.

'*Really?*' she asked, though she'd already made up her mind. True or not, she was going to believe it.

Clyde shrugged. 'It's what I heard. You'll never guess what else…'

Before Poppy knew it, she was smiling, then laughing. She might not have anything real to talk to Clyde about, but it was hilarious to hear conspiracies about their boss. Who cared if they were true?

After her fourth drink, a fifth and sixth materialised. Before long, the tingling around her temples became a buzzing and then, suddenly, she was grabbing Clyde's hand and pulling him onto the dance floor. She didn't know the track but it was something up-tempo and dancey: the exact thing Freya liked.

Poppy had never really been one for dancing but she knew more or less what to do. It was hard not to, when every other music video was of someone her age gyrating away.

Freya stepped out from behind the pillar, arms in the air and shouted a, 'Woo!' as she noticed Poppy. She wiggled her arse in Mark's direction but he was swaying, eyes glassy, struggling to keep his hands on her hips.

Clyde really *did* know how to dance. Poppy wasn't sure quite what he was doing, as her vision was starting to glaze. His legs were moving quickly, hips swaying, head bobbing.

'Woo!' Freya called, from the other side of the dance floor.

Poppy danced close to Clyde, letting him hold onto her waist, running her hand across his chest – which was so solid that she could feel his breastbone, his ribs, perhaps even his heartbeat.

It took her a few seconds to realise that the music had changed, the fizzing electronic beats seeping into something far slower. The pub had been empty but that was at least three drinks ago. Now, the dance floor was packed. Couples were closing in on one another: arms around necks; on waists, backsides, thighs.

The blinking, thumping strobes were now dizzying circles of light, making Poppy even more disorientated.

Clyde leaned in closely, lips almost brushing her ear. 'OK?'

Over his shoulder, Poppy saw Freya with both hands around Mark's neck. His hands were on her lower back and they were pressed together, nestling into one another.

Poppy reached forward and wrapped her hands around Clyde's waist, stepping in closer until her breasts were pushing on his chest. She rested her head on his shoulder, forcing him to hold her, and then started to bob from side to side. She could feel the sweat on his neck, could almost breathe it. It smelled of something rugged, something... She didn't know. It smelled of him.

Clyde had his hands on her bare back, fingers rubbing underneath her dress, close to her bra straps. Closer still. Touching the clasp. Brushing her hair. *In* her hair. Cupping her chin. Then he leaned back, forcing her to do the same. Moments later, his lips were on hers. They were much larger than hers but soft, too. He'd done this before. Perhaps a lot.

Poppy didn't care.

She closed her eyes and forced herself harder against him, raising her knee slightly and brushing his inner thigh. He clasped her even tighter than before. His tongue licked her top lip; she licked his.

And then she pulled away.

For a moment, she caught the confusion in Clyde's eyes, but then she hugged him tight, pressing onto the tips of her toes so she could just about see over his shoulder. He hugged her, thinking that was what she wanted.

In a way, it was.

Her eyes skirted past the throng of people, searching into the shadows, where Mark and Freya were still entwined with one another. Freya had her back to Poppy, and Mark's face was angled into the crook of her neck and shoulder.

His eyes were open, fixed on Poppy and Clyde. For a second, it felt like the room had stopped. People weren't dancing, the music wasn't playing, the lights weren't flickering. Poppy and Mark stared at each other, caught in the moment.

Then, as quickly as it had slowed, the room sped up again: music humming, people swaying, lights flaring.

Poppy blinked and then clamped her eyes closed. She twisted to nuzzle her lips into Clyde's sweat-soaked neck.

Nineteen

Poppy rubbed her tingling shoulder, wondering if she'd remembered to put suntan lotion on that bit. Sometimes, just sometimes, there was no other place on earth she'd rather be than Purley Green with a book on a sunny day.

She turned onto her back, pressing the irritable shoulder into the ground. The grass was a beautiful bright green, slightly springy because it hadn't been cut in a week. It tickled in a good way. She held her book high above her, using it to block the sun as she started to read.

She'd barely got through a paragraph when a shadow fell across her.

''Ello, stranger.'

Poppy pushed herself onto her elbows and squinted at the shape eclipsing the sun.

'Frey!'

She started to jump up but Freya was quicker. She dropped to her knees, wrapping her arms around Poppy. Moments later, they were rolling in the grass, giggling as if half their ages. When they eventually trundled to a stop, Poppy's ribs were sore from the laughing – and Freya's weight. There was grass in her hair, her top, her underwear, but she didn't care. They lay on their backs side by side, arms spread, staring up at the endless blue.

'I didn't think you'd be back this summer,' Poppy said, catching her breath.

'I had to come see my girlie on her birthday, didn't I?'

'What time did you get in?'

'Late last night. I got a lift off this lad, Ethan – but he was running late. He tried to floor it, 'cept the bizzies were out and about. He got pulled over for speeding. Three points probably. Bastards. We got here and then he carried on going to see his sister out Slough way.' A pause and then: 'Wherever that is.'

Poppy propped herself onto one elbow, staring down at her friend. Freya was wearing tiny denim hot pants that looked as if she'd cut them even shorter herself. The material of the pockets hung lower than the bottom of the shorts. On top, she had a spaghetti-strapped yellow vest that was cut low. The kinks of her dark hair were matted with grass, which she was picking out bit by bit.

'It is *so* good to see you, Pops,' Freya said, pushing herself onto an elbow, too. 'Happy birthday and all that, but, bloody hell, I don't know how you do it.'

'Do what?'

Freya sat up fully, holding her hands up to indicate the area around them. '*This*. Uni's amazing; the people are amazing; Plymouth's amayyyyyy-zing. Then I've got to come back to this sheeeeeeeet-hole.' She nodded her head decisively, as if hers was the only opinion on the matter.

Poppy took a breath. She wanted to disagree…

'How's the course?' she asked, instead.

Freya huffed and waved a dismissive hand in Poppy's direction. 'I don't worry 'bout it.'

She flopped back onto the grass. Poppy remained sitting.

'It's the first time I've seen you, since…' Poppy let the sentence hang, waiting for the response she'd been anticipating for months.

Freya's chest rose and fell with a sigh. 'I know I should've called you earlier, Pops, but it all happened so quickly. Mark and me were gonna do the whole long-distance thing but, well… It's a *long* way. Did he call you?'

'Not really.' A pause. 'Well… Sort of. A week or so after you.'

'What did he say?'

'Not much – just that you broke up over New Year. I've heard from him once or twice since then but we only talked about his uni stuff and what was going on here in Purley.'

Freya rolled onto her front and pulled down the straps of her top, exposing her shoulders. She twisted her face away from Poppy, leaving one cheek to face the sun.

'I went up to Manchester for Christmas, Pops. He kept going on about cooking us Christmas dinner. All his flatmates had gone home, so it was just him and me. It wasn't the same, though. I got back to Plymouth on New Year's Eve and phoned him to say it was done.'

Poppy paused to let this sink in. She'd heard bits and pieces over the past seven months but this sounded even more brutal than what she'd managed to piece together.

On the phone?

On New Year's Eve?

When Mark was by himself?

'What wasn't the same?' Poppy's voice was quieter than she'd expected, the words sticking in her throat.

'I didn't expect there to be so many cool people at uni, Pops. You're missing out, big time. It was an accident at first. There was this lad, Dean. I was pissed; he was pissed. You know how it goes.'

'*Dean?*' It was the first Poppy had heard of another guy.

'Yeah, you know…'

'Was that before or after you broke up with Mark?'

Freya rolled over and sat up. She and Poppy stared at one another and then Freya slowly pursed her lips. 'Has he been down this summer?'

Poppy shook her head.

'Is he coming down?'

Another shake. 'Not that he's told me.'

'I didn't know if he might be around today, what with your birthday and everything…'

Poppy had known her friend long enough to spot the glint in her eye. Freya *wanted* to see Mark – not to rekindle anything they'd once had, more for him to see her as she was now. She was wearing more make-up; her hair was bigger, clothing smaller. His feelings for her wouldn't have disappeared just like that, and she knew it. She wanted to see his reaction to the new Freya.

Freya took a small mirror from her bag to check she had removed all the pieces of grass from her hair. 'How's your fella?' she asked.

'Clyde?'

'Unless you've got another bloke on the go?'

'No, um… He's fine.' Poppy bit her lip, not quite sure what to add. 'It's our one-year anniversary today.'

Freya flashed a wicked grin over the mirror. 'Aye, aye. Filthy night in, is it? You lucky cow.'

'We're supposed to be going out as this joint anniversary-birthday thing later. Neither of us have much money, though, so I'm not sure what's going on. He's taking me somewhere as a surprise.'

There was another knowing smile from Freya, which was all the more annoying as it came from someone who knew nothing about the situation.

'He's probably gonna take you out for a quick Maccy D's,' Freya said, 'then straight home for some absolute dirt. Maybe he'll write you a song?'

Poppy rolled her eyes. 'If he goes anywhere near that guitar tonight, I'll shove it right up his…' She stopped herself, not wanting to talk about this now. 'I'll ask him to stop,' she concluded.

It was too late. Freya rocked back and forward with laughter, slapping her bare thigh. 'Not going well?'

Poppy sighed. 'It's not that, just…' Another sigh. 'He knows how to play "Knockin' On Heaven's Door" and he'll play these forty-five minute versions that make me want to rip my own ears off.'

Freya seemed distracted, staring past Poppy towards a pair of young teenage boys who were kicking a ball around on the far side of the green. The parish council had long ago banned ball games on the green but only the odd busybody seemed bothered about enforcing this.

'Look at the state of them,' Freya said.

Poppy peered towards the lads. 'What?'

'That's the standard of lads you have here. You should come to Plymouth, Pops. Lots of *proper* lads down there. Not boys: *men*, who make you shiver. Ooh, you'd love it.'

Poppy doubted that. She stared at the ground and started to pick at her shoelace. 'I'm kind of surprised that you and Mark…'

There was a silence that lasted too long. Poppy didn't dare look up.

'What you trying to say, Pops?' Freya said, eventually. She sounded close to one of her moods.

'I don't know.'

'Just cos you start going out with someone when you're a kid, it don't mean it's love forever.'

'I know; I didn't mean that.'

'I'm not making you pick between us,' Freya said. 'You can be friends with us both.'

Considering how infrequently she'd seen, texted, instant messaged, or spoken to Mark or Freya over the previous few months, Poppy wasn't sure she was friends with either of them.

Freya reached forward and pulled gently on Poppy's necklace. 'This is still lush,' she said.

'Thanks.'

'What did your old man get you for your birthday this year? A million quid?' Freya laughed but Poppy heard the edge, not doubting she was meant to.

Poppy shook her head. 'Some money. Not a million quid.'

Freya shrugged. 'Whatcha gonna get with it?'

'Food.'

'*Food?*' Freya stared at Poppy, as if the entire concept of using currency to pay for nourishment was something she'd never heard of. 'You still live at home, right?'

'Dad wanted me to pay rent but I don't make enough, so he has me buying my own food.'

'That's so tight.'

'I need some new work shoes, too. I might spend some of it on that.'

'Now we're talking.'

Poppy scooped her book into her bag. There was no chance of reading any more now.

Freya clipped her mirror shut and reburied it in her bag: 'You *are* coming down next year, aren't ya?'

'To Plymouth?'

'Where else?'

She made it sound like the centre of the world.

'I don't know. Maybe… Hopefully.'

She didn't sound hopeful but Freya wasn't listening anyway.

'I'm out of halls and living in a shared house next year, Pops. You can sleep on the floor by my bed. It's all girls.' She laughed. 'Well, it'll start as all girls. Who knows what'll happen when we hit the town?'

'I'll see how things go,' Poppy replied, knowing she definitely wouldn't visit. Sleeping on Freya's floor in a strange house, listening to the sound of other couples getting it on didn't seem that appealing.

'I'm going back down tomorrow,' Freya added. 'Don't want to miss a Friday night out, plus I only came back to say hi to Mum.' She paused. 'And for your birthday, of course.' She stopped briefly, then the verbal diarrhoea began again. 'Seriously, Pops. You should take your A levels again. They ain't that hard – I got two Cs and a D. Anyone can do it if I can. Come to uni. It's amazing.'

There was a big part of this suggestion that sounded appealing to Poppy. The idea of a life of few consequences; the parties and the new people. Even the idea of going to classes tempted her. Poppy was in a rut, working for very little money at the coffee shop, and spending all of it. A year had passed, yet little had changed. Mark and Freya had moved on and she hadn't. When she closed her eyes in bed some nights – when she thought too much about things, about how little she'd done – it actually hurt.

'I'm happy here,' Poppy said, trying to convince herself as much as her friend.

Freya fired straight back. 'What? Working in a coffee shop, living with your dad? You should—' Somehow, she managed to interrupt herself, barely pausing for breath, but slightly lowering her tone. 'Sorry, I didn't mean that.' Freya reached out and rested a hand on Poppy's knee. 'I'm worried about you, Pops. We've been friends for-*ev*-er. Ever and ever, like. I don't want to see you wasting your life.'

Poppy took Freya's hand and interlocked her fingers. Maybe Freya had meant to sound harsh; maybe she hadn't. Freya lived with a foot in her mouth. The two of them came from very different backgrounds. They had always enjoyed different interests but their friendship had remained strong. The past few months had pushed them apart. Poppy stood and pulled Freya to her feet. She stepped closer and wrapped her hands around her friend's clammy back.

'I've really missed you,' Poppy said.

'I've missed you, too, girlie.'

My dearest Poppy,

I hope you've forgiven me for ending my last letter on something of a cliffhanger. You will know bits and pieces anyway but I ended up taking the job with Mr Peters. It turned out that when I'd seen him every morning in the bakery, he'd been on his way to a manufacturing company that he owned and managed. It was based a little outside Ledford and produced sporting equipment for children. He wanted me to work as a salesperson.

When he explained that this meant visiting real, actual people and trying to sell them his products, my reaction was pure terror. I'd never done anything like that before. I was just nineteen years old and he wanted me to travel around the country to present products to older men and women – professionals, who worked as governors at schools, or had roles on local councils and the like.

I asked, 'Why me?' but all he said was that he knew I could do it.

I took the job, of course, primarily because I had no other option but also because I wanted to prove to him – and probably to myself – that I actually could do it.

I'm smiling as I write this – but I was really good at it. I had no particular training, other than learning what the products were, but somehow I knew what to say to people. Over the course of about a year, I brought in quite a lot of business – but that carried new expectations with it.

There was a big contract going for an entire school district in the Midlands. It was for around two hundred schools and worth a lot of money. Mr Peters said I was the person he wanted to make the sales pitch.

To say I was scared was an understatement.

I ended up travelling to meet this man who I'll call Mr K. We were in a side office of a hotel and it was all very cordial and professional. He was only a few years older than me but very charming and used to getting his own way.

I gave my presentation and he listened, then he told me he could get the same type of goods elsewhere for a lower price. He showed me a pair of catalogues from our rival companies and we began the process of haggling over the cost.

I'll save you the boring details but all this was very normal. We ended up having lunch at the hotel's restaurant, still talking over the pitch. Eventually, we got to the point where the offer he said was his 'final' one was still lower than the price I was allowed to sell the goods for.

I was pretty good at mental arithmetic and figured out that I could do the deal for the price he offered and dig into my own savings to make up the difference, knowing the commission I was due would replace my own money. With that, everyone would win. Mr K would get his goods at the price he wanted; Mr Peters would have an enormous new contract; I would have the glory of having made the deal.

Except I didn't do that – because Mr K's offer was not a fair one.

I believed in the products and that's what I said to Mr K. I told him he could pay less for inferior goods, but when they broke and needed to be replaced, his group of schools would have to pay out a second time. This was expensive stuff – climbing frames, football goals, things like that. He replied that what I said might be true – but he might not be doing the same job in years to come. In the short-term, he would still be the person who delivered on budget.

That was the point at which something snapped inside me. I remained calm on the outside but I was furious inside. Not because of the lost sale but because all these kids would be getting shoddy equipment and this man didn't seem to mind. So I told him that was fine – and that our price had gone up. It wasn't the price I'd quoted; it was that plus ten per cent.

You should have seen his face!

He said I was crazy, that this wasn't how business was done – but I picked up my things and told him it was no skin off my nose. I told him that I knew full well that of the companies bidding, we were the smallest. I was expected to come to this meeting and not make the sale. When I returned down south and told my company that the school district had gone somewhere else, no one would think any less of me. On the other hand, he was expected to make the right decision to benefit those kids. Perhaps he would leave the company in a year, or in five years. Maybe his decision wouldn't ever come back to bite him – but he would still know the truth of it. That he'd short-changed two hundred schools.

I picked up my things and I left.

This was before the days of mobile phones, so I was fuming the entire trip back to the office. You've probably figured out what happens next because, when I got there, we had the offer – including that extra ten per cent.

I learned a lot about people that day.

All sorts of scientists, philosophers and religious types have speculated about the meaning of life. It's one of those subjects that everyone thinks about at some point, even if it's only to ultimately dismiss it. My friend, Sharon, got into meditation at one point. She'd do it for hours. She'd tell us that she was in the process of reaching enlightenment and that when she discovered the meaning of life, she'd make sure she told us. As it happened, she ended up working on the checkout in Asda, which I don't think was much to do with the meditation. That said, perhaps it is the meaning of life. Who knows?

Truthfully, I'm not sure it really matters, but if life is about anything, then I think it's about the people with whom you surround yourself. Regardless of whether someone is friend or family, if they make you unhappy (truly unhappy, not just slam-a-few-doors unhappy because you're not allowed jelly for tea!), then you owe them nothing.

Your friendship is a privilege to them in the same way that theirs is to you. Never forget that. If you can, surround yourself with good people and enjoy the difference they make in your life. I only wish I'd learned that when I was younger.

I've always told you that I met your father at work. That is, of course, true, because I did meet Mr K again.

His name?

Christopher Kinsey.

Happy birthday,

Mum

A piece of gum was mushed into the cushion cover on the bench where Poppy was sitting. It was hard and no threat to her clothes – but it was still disgusting. What the hell was wrong with people?

'We can swap seats if you want?'

Clyde was trying to be nice. For the first time in a long time, he was wearing a shirt with *all* the buttons done up. He'd managed to find a pair of jeans that had no holes, and looked as smart as Poppy had seen him. She didn't want to say that she preferred him the way he usually was: in slouchy, baggy pants, with a loose top and his dreadlocks down. That was him; this was someone else.

The pub was very much them, though. Or it had *become* them over the past year. It was down the road from Clyde's flat, next to the bus stop and taxi rank. It was part of some identikit chain splattered around the country with cheap prices and dreadful microwaved food.

'I'm fine here,' Poppy replied, managing a thin smile.

Despite the heat of the day, it was freezing in the pub, and Poppy had not brought a coat. She was trying not to shiver in the short blue dress she was wearing – a dress she'd had since she was fifteen. She had thought about treating herself to something nicer with the birthday money from her dad – but the sobering reality of having to buy her own food had come first.

If she'd told her father how much she ended up spending on simply getting by, she was pretty sure he'd give her some leeway. He'd allow her to contribute less, leave her with a bit more to spend on herself – but her fear was that he'd ask her what she spent her money on. She knew that her father was trying to help, to teach her the value of money and hard work. If she told him how tight she was for cash, he might suggest putting together a budget, and then she'd know for sure how much she wasted in the pub and the café through the week.

Some things were better not knowing.

'You cold?' Clyde asked.

Poppy blinked back into the pub. 'No.'

'You were shivering.'

'No, I wasn't.'

'Right.'

Awkward silences were something Poppy and Clyde were incredible at. If there was ever an Olympic event that involved sitting close to another person while simultaneously struggling for something to say, the pair of them would take some beating. In fact, there was only one other thing they were exceptional at together – and that wasn't something they got up to in public.

'Takes a long time to get served in here, doesn't it?' Clyde said.

'Yeah, like the last time we were here.'

More silence.

Poppy didn't want to risk catching his gaze, so she picked up the drinks menu and peeped around it, taking in the rest of the pub. A gaggle of old blokes crowded the corner of the bar, drinking frothy pints of red-brown ale but not talking to each other. A little further on, younger lads huddled around a quiz machine, laughing and shouting as they tried to outwit it. On the other side of the bar, a group of couples had pushed three long tables together. At its head was a girl who looked around Poppy's age, wearing a paper party hat. There was a stack of presents beside her, next to a pile of cards. She was smiling, laughing, drinking. Enjoying her birthday.

Poppy's bag was buzzing, so she took out her phone with the hand that wasn't holding the menu and checked her messages underneath the table, away from Clyde's gaze. She bit the inside of her cheeks to stop herself from smiling.

Mark: 'Home! You free 2moz?'

Poppy: 'No :(Dad taking me away on Fri/Sat. Sun?'

She dropped the phone face-down on the bench next to her, then put the menu on the table.

'You all right?' Clyde asked, nodding at the bench and her phone.

'Just Dad making sure I'm all right.'

Clyde looked over his shoulder towards the bar. 'This food is taking forever.'

'Right…'

'You want another drink?' Clyde cupped his hand around an invisible glass and tilted it back and forth: universal sign language.

'Same again,' Poppy replied. Pints of lager were the only things that were going to get her through the night.

As Clyde stood, Poppy's phone buzzed again.

Mark: 'Can't – M&D got me visiting family etc. Here, there, everywhere! Wk on Fri?'

Poppy: 'Can't – work all day, then busy. When else are you free?'

Poppy left the screen illuminated, hoping Mark would reply quickly, but Clyde returned before a text arrived. He was expertly carrying four pints and placed them carefully on the table.

'Figured we wouldn't have to go back so quickly,' he said.

'Right… Thanks.'

Poppy downed the rest of the one she was drinking and then shifted two of the glasses towards her.

'Barman knew my order,' Clyde said.

'Oh, that's um… Good.'

Another pause and then: 'I told him it was your birthday.'

'Why?'

Clyde shrugged. 'Dunno. In case he wanted to give you something for free.'

'Did he?'

'No.'

'Great.'

Clyde sipped the top of his drink and Poppy did the same. She had no idea what to say and even less idea how they'd managed to maintain this over the course of a year. She'd not spoken to Freya in months, not seen her in even longer, yet their instant bond always gave them something to talk about. With Clyde, however, there was nothing.

They were together because the alternative was loneliness. Freya and Mark had gone and Clyde was all she had.

Mark: 'Now?'

Poppy stared at the single word beaming up at her. The tingle along her back was so intense that she had to fight to stop herself from turning to see if there was anyone behind her. She locked the screen and dropped it into her bag, peering up and catching Clyde's stare.

'I'm going to go,' she said firmly.

He said nothing at first but then his face fell. The bright toothy smile was a thing of the past. 'We can go somewhere else if you're sick of waiting for the food…?'

'It's not the food.'

Clyde's head dipped slightly and he took a breath. 'I know it would've been better if we'd gone to a proper restaurant. I'm a bit short this month and—'

'It's not this place, either. Not really. It's…'

Poppy stopped herself as a stooped woman arrived with a pair of plates. She placed the mixed grill in front of Clyde and the chicken curry in front of Poppy, then muttered something about sauces before disappearing back towards the bar. Poppy didn't touch her cutlery, or the food. She looked down at the plate, where the sauce was congealing with the rice. An unhealthy-looking oil was creeping towards the edge of the plate. She could feel Clyde staring at her.

'Do you think this is working?' she asked, looking up again.

The whites of Clyde's eyes were wide and round. 'I… Well… It's because we've not been able to get our own place, isn't it? We never get time alone and we're working together every day.'

Poppy shook her head. 'It's not that. It's me.' She stood and looped her bag over her shoulder. 'I'll quit the café, too. You play gigs there. I won't make it awkward. I'll call Mr C tomorrow – either that, or I'll go in early before you get there.'

Clyde was still staring at her, any pretence of coolness gone. 'Is it about the meal?'

'No.'

'Something I said?'

'No – it's me. I don't want whatever this is.'

Poppy waited for a moment, wondering if Clyde would add anything. Deep down, he must know that what she was saying was true.

When he didn't reply, Poppy stepped away from his outstretched arm and bounded towards the door. Anything Clyde might have said as she walked away was drowned out by the rampant *ding-dinging* of the nearby fruit machine paying out. Poppy didn't turn and she didn't stop walking.

It was so quiet that Poppy's knock echoed around the street. She could sense curtains twitching, neighbours nosing, beaks being poked in. Village-types lived for this sort of late-night drama. She bounced on the balls of her feet before deciding that this wasn't a good idea in the heels she was wearing. She took her phone out of her bag and then returned it. No missed calls, no messages.

Hopefully, Clyde understood.

She'd not woken up that morning trying to think of the best way to be an utter cow – who did? – but she'd sure as hell managed it. She had been snarky with Freya, horrible to her dad and even worse to Clyde. He'd changed so much over the past year: from the laid-back, smiling person he once was, to an awkward, unsure-what-to-say stammerer.

She'd done that to him – and he'd done the same to her.

Loneliness had destroyed them, and they'd destroyed each other. At least they weren't forty and washed up, stuck in a relationship they each resented, staying together for the kids. She was only nineteen. *Newly* nineteen. This was better for both of them. Clyde would understand in time. It had taken Poppy long enough to understand it herself.

The door opened, revealing Mr Ellery in a long, lime-green dressing gown that he was mercifully clutching together at the waist. His hair was grey, muscles not as defined, but Mark's father was undoubtedly a taller version of his son. They shared the same square jaw and angled cheekbones. Even their voices were similar: deep but kindly.

Mr Ellery took a small step back when he spotted Poppy in her short dress and heels. 'Oh… Poppy…' he said, before catching himself and checking his watch. 'We weren't expecting you…'

'Is Mark in?'

Mark's father eyed her again before nodding and stepping back into the house. Poppy heard Mark's name being called, then the sound of feet on steps. Moments later, he was in front of her: bare-footed, skinnier than she remembered, unshaven, hair a mess of sticky-out bits.

'Pops,' he said, blinking.

'You asked if I was free tonight.'

'You never texted back. I thought—' He stopped himself and eyed Poppy's feet. 'Did you walk here in those?'

Poppy shook her head: 'Taxi from Ledford to Purley. The first one didn't arrive, the second got lost. Long story.'

'Right… It's half-ten. What do you want to do?'

She shrugged. 'Go for a walk.'

'In *those* shoes?'

Poppy bent down and scooped the first heel from her foot, wobbling awkwardly from side to side. 'I can do bare feet.'

'You sure?'

'It's a superpower that only women have.'

Mark seemed understandably confused, but he popped inside to tell his parents he was going out. When he re-emerged, he was still bare-footed. 'Anything you can do,' he said.

They headed along the garden path onto the pavement in the general direction of the village centre. With their bare feet, they moved slowly, 'eep'ing and 'ouch'ing as they trod on small stones. The sky had started to turn a dusky purple but it wasn't quite dark. The heat of the day had crept into the night. Poppy wasn't cold, even in her short dress.

She told Mark about her nightmare taxi journey from Ledford, leaving out the fact that the reason she'd been in Ledford was that she'd skipped out on a meal with her now ex-boyfriend. Mark talked about his journey down from Manchester on the train, somehow making it sound interesting. He'd been confused by the electric sliding door of the toilet, thinking it was locked when it wasn't. Then an old woman had sat next to him and spent an hour talking about conspiracy theories. He'd been too polite to put his earphones in. Before long, Poppy and Mark were reminiscing about rowdy bus journeys they'd taken for days out in the city. Conversation was easy. They spoke the same language.

They were soon at Purley Green, the grass providing a soft cushion for their feet. Poppy headed for one of the benches and sat down. Mark was next to her, not touching, but close enough that she could feel the heat of his arms. The area was illuminated by the moon as the deep orange on the horizon finally faded to black.

'I was here with Frey earlier,' Poppy said.

Mark's voice was calm. 'I didn't know she was home.'

'She's going back to Plymouth tomorrow. Only came up for my birthday.'

'That's nice.'

'Yeah…'

Poppy didn't elaborate because she could sense Mark was wanting to speak. He shifted his weight forward on the bench, resting his elbows on his knees and rubbing his temples.

'I'm sorry I didn't call you more,' he whispered. It took Poppy a moment to figure out what he'd said because his words were so soft that they were almost swallowed by the night.

'It's OK,' she replied, not meaning it.

'I knew there was something wrong when Frey came up for Christmas. We had my whole place to ourselves and there was loads going on outside. Christmas markets, events, all sorts – but she didn't want to do anything. We stayed in and watched TV most days. In the evening, she was only interested in going to the local pub. We had a few drinks, then she grumbled when I wanted to go home. She'd gone back to Plymouth for New Year's, but on New Year's Eve we'd agreed to get back to the house to Skype at midnight. She texted me at about five, though, asking me to call – then said there was too much going on in her life and that she didn't have time for a long-distance relationship.'

He allowed his head to flop forward, staring at the ground.

'You could've called,' Poppy said quietly. 'Or Skyped, or texted.'

'I know… I sort of buried myself in uni work. Then I knew you'd have heard anyway and I was embarrassed for not being in contact sooner, so I left it even longer. I thought you'd hate me for not telling you.'

'No, you didn't.'

Mark glanced sideways at her, tongue cocked on his bottom row of teeth. He sighed. 'You're right – I didn't.'

They sat saying nothing for a few moments, listening to the glorious silence of the night.

'What do you think now?' Poppy asked.

Mark pressed back on the bench, feet stretched in front of him, using the big toe on his left foot to flick away flecks of grit from his right foot. 'I suppose I thought it was fair enough. At least she was honest, rather than stringing me along until Easter or the summer. I guess it was more the shock. We'd been together since we were fourteen; we'd known each other since we were six. I didn't see it coming at all.'

'I thought you'd end up getting married: house, big car, kids, and all that.'

It took a while for the reply to come. When it did, it wasn't exactly what Poppy expected. 'I'm not sure if we were ever really suited, if I'm honest. You know when you keep doing something because it's the easy thing to do…? It was like that. Perhaps Freya was the smart one to realise it.'

There was silence as a cloud passed in front of the moon, temporarily leaving them in darkness. This silence wasn't awkward like the pauses Poppy endured with Clyde. It was full of understanding – each of them waiting patiently in case the other wanted to add anything. Poppy found herself fiddling with her necklace: a habit she had developed over the past year. She straightened it, and then, as the cloud continued on its merry way, it was as if the lights had been switched on. In the moonlight, Poppy could see that there was something on the bench between herself and Mark that hadn't been there before.

'I wrapped it myself,' Mark said.

The small rectangle was wrapped in silver paper, with pink ribbons and a bow to finish it off.

'Sure it wasn't wrapped by your mum?' Poppy asked, picking up the gift.

'All me.'

Poppy tugged the ribbon until it slipped away and then ran her finger underneath the paper join to open it up. Inside was another tin of pencils.

'Ta-da!' Mark said.

'Hardly a surprise, is it?' Poppy said, smiling.

'Disappointed?'

Poppy put a hand on top of his. 'Never.' She put the gift and wrapping into her bag and stood. 'Let's keep walking.'

They continued across the grass and over the cobbles, wincing, hopping and giggling until they made it to the safety of the other side. Poppy stopped outside a shop window and pressed her forehead to the glass.

'It's so weird to see all the shops without metal shutters at night,' Mark said. 'You get used to it in the city. It gets dark and the shutters come down, or the glass is lined with that wire mesh. It's so unfriendly, not like here…' He touched the glass with his hand, as if to convince himself it was real.

The lack of shutters wasn't something Poppy had ever noticed before. She'd been in cities late at night, of course. She had seen shuttered shops and all the scruffy posters attached to the front – but it had only ever been a night here and there. Purley was her normality.

'I can't believe Mrs Dowson's Sweets is still going,' Mark said.

Poppy couldn't disagree. 'I used to spend all my pocket money in here,' she replied.

'So did I. Do you remember, she used to have this massive tub behind the counter? It was filled with those chocolate button things covered in hundreds and thousands. They were two pence each and I'd buy a quid's worth at a time.'

'I always bought the sherbet dips,' Poppy said. 'Or Caramacs. I bloody loved Caramacs – can't remember the last time I had one. Mum used to stand in the doorway while I was deciding and tell me to get a shift on.'

An image of this appeared so clearly in Poppy's mind that she shivered. She was a little girl again, running her hand along the front of the sweet tubs, trying to decide what she wanted, breathing in the smell of sugar, sherbet and liquorice. Mrs Dowson was behind the counter, smiling and indulgent, but Poppy's mother was at the door, checking the time and tapping her foot.

Poppy placed a hand on the shop door now, remembering how her mum would eventually say she was going – and that if Poppy didn't get on and pay, then she'd get nothing.

She shivered again. Mark noticed this time, placing a hand on her shoulder.

'It's OK to miss her,' he said.

Poppy reached into her bag and removed the envelope with her mum's writing on the front. She passed it to Mark, who traced the letters of Poppy's name with his hand, before turning it over and handing it back.

'What's this – a birthday card?' he asked. 'Why are you carrying it around?'

'Before she died, my mum wrote me a letter for each of my next ten birthdays. This is number four.'

His eyes widened with surprise. 'Oh.'

'Every year, I look forward to reading the new one, like it's going to be my best present, and then, afterwards… I don't know. Sometimes I wish she'd never written them.'

Mark's hand was on her bare shoulder again, pulling her closer to him. 'Why?'

She shrugged. A lump was forming in her throat. Why had she started telling him this? 'Because I wish she was here. Every time I read her letters, I wonder what she might be doing if she were still alive.'

'What are they about?'

Poppy shook her head.

'What were the last three about?'

'Things… Stories. Advice. She'd never have told me all this in person because I wouldn't have listened. It feels different when it's written down.'

Poppy pulled her bag higher on her shoulder and looped her arm through Mark's. She gave him her shoes to carry, and before they knew it, they were heading towards the bridge – Purley Hill beyond, and Poppy's home. They walked slowly, not saying much, but not needing to. Mark was the only person she'd ever told about the letters. He didn't ask any more about it, perhaps sensing that she'd already said everything she wanted to.

By the time they reached the path that led to Poppy's front door, she was feeling self-conscious about the fact she still lived at home. Mark was off in Manchester, Freya in Plymouth. But here Poppy was, newly nineteen and in the same bedroom she'd always had.

'What's wrong?' Mark asked, when she stopped.

Poppy turned to look up at her bedroom window, making sure he couldn't see her features. 'You've all moved on without me.'

Mark let go of her arm and slipped his hand around her hip, slightly cupping her belly. He was so close to her now that she could feel his reply tickling her ear. 'Everyone's different, Pops. If we all did A levels and went to uni to do the same course, it'd be a pretty boring world.'

'That's easy to say when you're the one who escaped.'

'If you want to leave, then what are you waiting for? You've been working for the past year and a bit. You might not have much but you must have *some* money. You could pack a bag and go anywhere you want. Rent a flat, meet new people, do what you want for a while. If it all goes to shite, at least you've always got a home. Some people don't have that.'

Poppy rested back into him, her head underneath his chin. She could feel his heart beating. '*Shite?*' she said.

His chest bobbed with a laugh. 'You pick up words like that, living in Manchester. Eh, our kid?' He breathed out and then added. 'You're unique, Pops. You're you. I like you the way you are.'

Poppy twisted to face him. Mark's hand stayed a little above her hips. She could feel the warmth of his fingers through her dress. His index finger was gently rubbing up and down, making her tingle. She stared up at him, taking in the moonlit freckles across the top of his nose.

'Hi,' she said.

'Hi.'

She wasn't sure if she leaned in first, or if Mark did, but the result was the same. The next thing she knew, their lips were on one another's. The kiss didn't have the same passion and fury as the ones she'd shared with Clyde. It was slower, more tender. She could actually *feel* it.

Poppy might not have known who leaned in first, but it was definitely Mark who pulled away. He was smiling sadly, his gaze still locked onto her. She could see the moon in his eyes.

'Sorry,' he whispered.

His fingers loosened and she knew that was it. No point in pressing forward, or in trying to pull him to her. One word had done it.

After all those years of being two-plus-one, it was hard to be anything other than the one. Poppy pictured Freya's reaction if Mark and Poppy ever became a thing. They'd be 'PopMark', which even sounded like some sort of disease.

She wondered if Freya was who Mark was thinking of. They might have broken up but they'd been together for years before that. Did he see Poppy as the 'plus one'…?

'I'm sorry, too,' Poppy said, trying to maintain some degree of dignity.

Mark took another step away, arms by his side, then behind his back. His stare was unbroken. 'I should go.'

'Goodnight, then.'

Two more steps, and then he turned and started to walk back towards the village, bare feet soundless on the pavement. Poppy watched, wanting to say something, to call him back and say that *she* wasn't sorry at all. But half a dozen more steps and the shadow of a nearby hedge swallowed him whole. Poppy continued to watch, suddenly feeling a cold she wasn't sure was to do with the night.

Then she turned to head into the house.

Twenty

Poppy had only taken a single step away from the train when somebody shunted into her shoulder. She was thrust sideways as she heard a muttered, 'Sorry,' but the figure was already disappearing into the throng of people. She wasn't even sure if it had been male or female.

After straightening herself, Poppy hoisted her camping rucksack higher on her shoulders, but it was heavy and ridiculously unwieldy. She was struggling to balance herself with the pack on her back, and as she turned to look for the exit, she accidentally bumbled into a young woman who was about her own age. The other woman was talking into her mobile phone, and the interruption only broke her flow in the sense that it made her scowl as she continued speaking. Poppy mumbled her own apology and then began to weave her way through the horde towards the exit sign.

She'd been to Bristol and Cardiff on the train before. She had been places she thought were busy – but had never seen so many people crowded into such a small space as this. There were entire families of adults and kids hauling gigantic suitcases behind them as they trekked towards the exit, not to mention the couples, singles, and groups of lads and girls. Everywhere Poppy looked, there were heads bobbing along the platform.

'Pops!'

Poppy stopped on the spot and pushed herself onto tiptoes, trying to peer over the people around her. That was all well and good, but because of the backpack, her abrupt movement, and a niggly little thing called gravity, all she succeeded in doing was overbalancing. Luckily, a tall man in a suit was striding – or trying to stride – behind her. As she started to topple backwards, he shunted her forwards again with his forearm and a tut, rocking her back into position.

She called another apology after him, but he was already on his way, newspaper clamped under his arm, briefcase in hand.

'Pops!'

The voice was closer this time, and before Poppy knew it, there were arms around her. She wasn't quite sure how it happened, considering the rucksack was only a small step away from a straitjacket, but in one swift movement it was off her back and over Mark's shoulder.

'Welcome to Blackpool,' he said.

Since she'd last seen him, Mark had allowed his stubble to grow out into a neatly trimmed beard. His hair was shorter, between the scraggly unkemptness of the previous summer and the buzz cut he'd had growing up. It took Poppy a few seconds to take him in because it was a lot to absorb. It was as if he'd grown into his face over the past twelve months. As if this was the height and weight he'd now be forever.

In the scrum of him taking her bag, Poppy realised too late that she still had a hand on his forearm. She felt the muscle flex as he turned and nodded at the woman standing behind him.

'This is Iris,' he said. 'First, let's get out of here.'

Without waiting for them, Mark led a way through the crowd. It was like Moses parting the Red Sea as people moved aside to let him through. He was moving so quickly that Poppy had to skip the first few steps to stay in his wake.

'How was your journey?' Iris asked.

Poppy glanced at her quickly, not wanting to make it look like she was having a proper peek, even though she was.

Iris was the same age as Poppy, with a long gypsy skirt down to her ankles and a loose white top that exposed tanned golden arms. Her hair was in the flimsiest of ponytails, and was a sort of browny-mahogany colour with a slight wave and glimmering highlights that either meant she spent hours at a time in a salon, or that she was one lucky so-and-so.

'Long,' Poppy replied, trying not to shout even though she wanted to be heard over the crowd. 'I had to get a taxi to Temple Meads, then a train to Birmingham, another to Preston, then this one to Blackpool. The toilets were closed on the second train, so, er...'

Poppy realised belatedly that nobody wanted to hear about the state of the toilets, let alone someone she'd just met. She wasn't making the best of first impressions.

Iris thankfully didn't reply because Mark had reached the station doors. They slipped through a gap between a pair of lads wearing England football tops, and then they were on a large paved area with a rank of taxis ahead. Mark kept walking until he was next to a large red-brick wall and the crowd had finally started to peter out.

He put Poppy's bag on the ground and then stretched high, cricking his back. 'What have you got in there?' he asked.

'Stuff.'

'Like dead bodies or something? It weighs a ton.'

Poppy nudged him with her elbow. 'You know I gave up murdering people years ago.'

They grinned at one another and, for a moment, it was just the two of them again. Teenagers once more, all knowing looks and age-old in-jokes.

'Where are you staying?' Iris asked.

The spell was broken and Poppy fiddled with her phone to find the bed and breakfast's confirmation email, before copying and pasting the address into the maps app. In theory, modern technology was a wonderful time-saver. In practice, she only had a single bar of signal and could have probably thrown a stone in a random direction and found the place quicker.

When the page had finally loaded, it took the three of them nearly five minutes to figure out where their three-dimensional selves were in relation to the two dimensions of the map.

They stood in a line, pointing in various directions, saying things like, 'Is that left?' while pointing right and then indicating the other way and querying whether there were perhaps two lefts. The low point came when Poppy queried whether the train station was in front of them, when it was clearly at their backs. It didn't say much for the British educational system but, eventually, they managed to navigate the half-dozen streets necessary to get Poppy checked into her B&B.

Free of her bag, the three of them headed back towards the centre of Blackpool. Mark and Iris held hands, with Poppy walking beside them. Old habits died hard, she thought, remembering how often she had walked like this beside Mark and Freya. Forever the one.

'What I don't get,' Poppy said, 'is why we're not doing this in Manchester?'

Mark and Iris exchanged a knowing look that said they'd had this conversation already. Iris unexpectedly reached out and took Poppy's hand, and the three of them walked in tandem. 'We figured that if we were going to take you out and show you the north of England, that we might as well go to the seaside for a few days.'

Poppy had to let go of Iris's hand as they reached a family with a push-chair. The streets were becoming busier as they neared the shore, the noise rising too. When they were clear of the family, Poppy wasn't sure whether to offer her hand again, so she held it by her side, feeling a bit strange.

'What do you reckon so far?' Iris asked.

'It's busy,' Poppy replied.

'I've never seen so many people here,' Iris replied. 'Every time I've visited, it's been quiet. Must be because the sun's out.'

Iris was right about that. Yet again, the sun was blessing Poppy's birthday with its presence. It had been warm down south but Black-pool could've been mistaken for the tropics, given the weather. There would be newspaper reports somewhere declaring Britain warmer than Spain, as if it were a competition. As if anyone in Spain cared.

The three of them crossed the road and approached the wall on the far side of the promenade, giving Poppy her first view of the sea up north. It looked wrong. Instead of the blue waves that smashed onto the southern coast, here they were a murky blue-brown, with lengthy ripples of dirty white foam splashing across the top. The beach itself was more people than sand: a kaleidoscope of blankets, deckchairs and windbreakers stretching as far as Poppy could see. Stunted fairground music spilled from the nearby pier, with an undercurrent of arcade machine dings seep-ing onto the street. The promenade was heaving, too. A large group of topless men ambled past, reddened burnt bellies hanging over the top of baggy swim shorts as they called across the street to a group of women in bikinis and sandals. Poppy didn't know where to look. There was more to see in a few square metres here than there was in the entirety of Purley.

Mark sat on a wall, legs dangling down towards the beach as he stared out at the ocean. Iris sat down next to him, Poppy on the other side. They were quiet for a moment, watching the mass of humanity below. Poppy focused on a woman who was banging a bottle of suntan lotion with her hand, simultaneously bellowing a string of expletives in the direction of what were presumably her kids.

'I've heard loads about you,' Iris said, leaning forward slightly to talk to Poppy across Mark. Poppy eyed her, looking for sarcasm or an undercurrent of tension. There was nothing: Iris was being nice. 'I've been looking forward to meeting Mark's friends,' she added.

'Here I am,' Poppy replied, unsure what else to say.

Mark began to tell the story of how he and Poppy had met in primary school and how they'd been friends ever since. 'Back then,' he said, 'it was all about knocking on each other's front door to see if the other person wanted to come out and play. Now it's instant messages, texts and the odd email!'

Poppy laughed along with him. He was right. She couldn't remember the last time they'd actually spoken – phone calls seemed so ancient. Instead, they fired messages and pictures of pugs and cute kittens back and forth. The moment between them from the previous year, the kiss on her doorstep, had never been mentioned again. Poppy sometimes wondered if she'd dreamt it. She was too scared to ask why he'd pulled away.

As Mark continued to tell the story of their friendship, Poppy filled in the odd blank. She'd not thought about those early days in a long while. Iris nodded along, laughing in all the right places and, before long, the pair of them were teasing Mark about the flares he used to wear. He eventually threw his hands in the air, grinning. 'I'm sick of you ganging up on me,' he said. 'I'm off to get some chips.'

As soon as he said it, Poppy realised the air was drenched in the scent of salt, vinegar and frying potatoes. Her mouth began to water and her stomach rumbled.

If the sea was a disappointment, then the chips were a revelation. Purley had a single chippy, not far from the green, but the food it sold was like sweaty flip-flops compared to this. Poppy's chips were mushed together into a wonderful potatoey mass alongside a piece of fish so big that it was more like a mini shark. She had got a strange look from the man behind the counter for asking what a barm was, before finding out that it was a giant bread roll. She wondered if everyone knew that, or if it was only her who'd somehow missed the day at school where they talked through names for bread.

Mark led them back to the wall and they sat down as a trio, poking away at their dinner with wooden forks that brought a new definition to the word blunt.

'Like being at home for you, this, isn't it?' Mark said to Iris.

She had a mouthful of fish but nodded.

'Iris is from Whitby,' Mark explained. 'Her parents run a café out there.'

Poppy didn't want to ask where Whitby was, assuming it was a seaside resort somewhere. It dawned on her how little she knew about the country she lived in. She knew Bristol well enough and had been to Weston-Super-Mare and Weymouth, though not often. They were nearby beaches, which was reason enough. Other than that, she knew little past the boundaries of where she lived.

She felt so very small.

'What are you studying at Manchester?' Poppy asked.

'Business management,' Iris replied. Poppy was embarrassed to realise she didn't know what that meant. She knew the words separately, of course, but did 'business management' mean Iris was studying to be a manager of a specific business, or was it the theory of business and finance itself? Was there a difference? Poppy didn't know and didn't want to ask for fear of looking stupid. It felt as if Mark and Iris lived in a world separate to her own, in which she was too dim to partake. She felt as if she was shrinking in front of them.

She chewed on a smushed chip and nodded thoughtfully, as if it all made perfect sense.

'Did Mark tell you how we met?' Iris asked, thrusting her wooden fork in the air, a chip impaled on the prongs.

Poppy stared out towards the horizon, where blue met blue and there was only a fuzzy dark line to separate them. 'Go on,' she said, meaning, 'please don't'.

Iris ate the chip, which was her last, and then screwed up the paper, tossing it into the nearby bin. She even had good aim, Poppy thought.

'We both live in the same block of private halls,' Iris said. 'Everyone has their own bathroom and bedroom but there are half a dozen shared kitchens on each floor. The place is massive. I'd gone down to the ground floor to pick up my mail. There's this big post box area with hundreds of cubbyholes. People can pick up their post whenever they remember. It's usually only junk mail – pizza menus, that kind of thing. Anyway, when I got back to my room, I realised I'd locked myself out. It was gone ten o'clock—'

'Ten at night?' Poppy interrupted.

'Right, ten at night. The management company can send someone to let you back in but there's a call-out charge if it's after ten and I didn't have my phone anyway – it was locked in my room. So, I'm sitting in the corridor not sure what to do. No one's in sight and it's getting later. It's gone eleven and I'm wondering if I'll have to sleep in the hallway.' Iris nudged Mark with her shoulder. 'Luckily, this lump shows up. He's been working late in the library and has to walk past me to get to his door. Turns out we only live four doors apart but we've never seen or spoken to each other because we share different kitchens. He invites me in for a brew and then we sit up half the night talking. One thing leads to another and here we are.'

Iris was dangling her legs over the wall, swinging them back and forth. As she finished telling the story, she reached out and interlocked her fingers with Mark's. She gazed at him wide-eyed and then rested her head on his shoulder.

'That's a good story for the grandkids,' Poppy said, only half joking.

'Do you have a boyfriend?' Iris asked.

Poppy wanted Iris to have an edge, for this question to be a dig. She wanted to dislike her, but it seemed that Iris was genuinely making an effort to get to know her boyfriend's oldest friend.

'I was seeing someone last year but it didn't work out,' Poppy replied. 'I moved to Bristol about three months ago and got a new job. There are lots of new people around me now, so we'll see.'

'What do you do?'

Poppy hated this question but offered her standard response – the one she gave her father every time he asked. 'It's database stuff, filling in forms online and the like.'

Iris hummed a neutral response, which was fine by Poppy – better than the 'Oh, that sounds interesting,' that usually came from people who clearly thought differently. Poppy was well aware that her job *didn't* sound interesting, largely because it wasn't. The description she gave offered just enough to stop people questioning her. 'Database stuff' could mean anything. She could be cataloguing terrorist weapons for all anyone else knew.

'There's lots of in-house training,' Poppy added, speaking too quickly. This was her standard justification for doing the job. 'A proper structure to work your way up and lots of chance for advancement…' Poppy pinched the skin on the back of her hand. This corporate nonsense was annoying even her, yet it kept coming.

'There's discounted gym membership…' Which she didn't use. 'Safe bicycle parking and showers on site…' Which she didn't use. 'There's a staff loyalty scheme where you get discounts in local shops…' Which she didn't use. 'Plus they have a private health scheme…' Which she couldn't afford. 'So, there's loads going on.'

Iris's head was still resting on Mark's shoulder but nodding in agreement. Mark was staring out towards the ocean, either not taking it in, or seeing right through the upbeat baloney Poppy had been spouting.

'Poppy draws, too,' Mark said unexpectedly.

Iris leaned forward to peer around Mark. 'You're an artist?'

'Well, I only—'

'She's *really* good,' Mark added.

'I'm not that good; I sketch a bit.'

Mark flipped his legs back over the wall until he was facing the promenade instead of the beach. The other two followed his lead and then he held out an expectant hand. Iris reached into her bag and passed over a small rectangle that was wrapped neatly in green paper covered by teddy bears.

'Speaking of which,' Mark said, passing the gift to Poppy. 'I wrapped this one, too.'

She wasn't sure she believed him, but she pulled the paper apart without questioning him further, unveiling the familiar set of pencils. 'Surprise,' she said.

'I told you I was going to keep buying you a set every year.'

'I've not used last year's much,' Poppy ran her fingers across the smooth tin. 'Sorry…'

Iris's expertly manicured eyebrows were drawn downwards. 'You get Poppy the same present every year?'

Mark started to dig around his pockets until he emerged with his phone. He flicked across the screen and then held it up for Iris to see. 'Pops drew this when we were thirteen.'

Iris took the phone and stared at it. 'That's *really* good.' She looked up to Poppy. 'This is great.' She turned the device around to show the photograph Mark had taken of one of Poppy's drawings.

It was a simple sketch of Poppy, Mark and Freya: nothing special and barely even shaded. She'd done it during a maths lesson one freezing December afternoon and then signed it for Mark – back in the days when that had seemed like a fun thing to do. She remembered how she used to practise autographs for when she got famous – a prospect which was looking less and less likely. To be famous, a person generally had to achieve something – even if it was taking their top off on late-night Channel Five. Poppy hadn't even managed that.

She shrugged, embarrassed, though also wondering what Iris might make of Freya. Surely she knew Freya was Mark's ex? If she was concerned that he was keeping a sketch of his former girlfriend on his phone, then she didn't show it.

'Why haven't you been drawing this year, Pops?' Mark asked, putting his phone away. He sounded stern, like a teacher.

'Time.'

'Weren't you between jobs for a while?'

'That's a kind way of saying I was scrounging.'

Mark frowned at her. 'No one thinks you were scrounging, Pops. You left one job and, after a while, you started a new one. I'm only asking why you didn't use those pencils in between times.'

Poppy stared at her feet, chastened. 'It didn't feel right,' she said.

'But you are going to start again this year, aren't you?'

'There's a gallery close to my new flat that hosts weekly classes, so… Maybe.'

Mark rubbed her shoulder. 'I'll take a maybe.'

Poppy was saved from any further grilling by the buzzing of her phone. She expected it to be her dad, making sure she'd arrived safely, but when she looked, it was Freya's name on the screen. She thought about rejecting the call, but knew her friend would call straight back. And then call again and again. She'd keep dialling until Poppy answered. It was the Freya way.

'Be right back,' Poppy told Mark and Iris, and then started towards a row of benches that were being used as a climbing frame by a trio of skinny, topless young boys.

'Hello,' Poppy said, finger in her opposite ear to block out the noise.

'What's she like then?' Freya replied, short and direct.

'Sorry? Who?'

'Who'd you think? That tart Mark's shacked up with.'

'Oh, Iris.'

Freya mimicked Poppy's voice: '*Oh, Iris.* That's one of the stupidest names I've ever heard. What is she, like, ninety years old?'

Poppy was a good twenty metres away from Iris and Mark but lowered her voice anyway. 'No, she's kind of… Normal.'

'*Normal?*'

'What do you want me to say?'

There was a bang from the other end of the line and Freya swore under her breath. 'Hang on.' The line went quiet for a few seconds, in which time Poppy offered a smile and nod in Mark's direction to let him know she was fine. There was a second bang and then Freya started to speak again, acting as if nothing had happened.

'What's she *actually* like, then? I've seen some pictures online but they look Photoshopped. She fat? Ugly? There was this one photo where it looked like she had a scar on her cheek, but it might've been a shadow.'

Poppy squinted towards Iris, though she had no idea why. She knew exactly what she looked like. 'She's not fat or ugly, Frey. She's normal.'

'She must be a bitch though, right? Making sarky comments and all that.'

'No, she's been really nice and welcoming.'

'*Nice?* Whose side are you on?' Freya was shouting.

'I'm not on anyone's side, Frey. I've come up to Blackpool for a weekend away.'

There was a pause and then a huff so loud that Poppy had to move the phone away from her ear.

'I've gotta go, Pops. Things to see, people to do… No, I mean… Well, whatever. Happy birthday and all that.'

'Thanks, I er—' Poppy stopped because the line was dead. She sighed. This was Freya all over – she didn't want Mark but didn't want anyone else to have him, either. Perhaps that was why Mark had pulled away from Poppy a year ago. Freya's reaction to them getting together would have been unpredictable at best, volcanic at worst. Best friends didn't do that sort of thing to one another.

Poppy re-pocketed her phone and then headed back to the wall, where Mark was sitting by himself. 'Where's Iris?' she asked.

Mark nodded towards the nearby pier. 'Gone to find a toilet.'

'Right...' Poppy sat next to him but it didn't feel right sitting too close without Iris on the other side. 'Thanks for inviting me up,' she said.

'Iris's idea – she wanted to meet you.'

'Oh.'

'She's really great, Pops.'

'I know.'

He rocked his shoulder into hers. 'You and me will always be mates.'

'Right... *Mates.*'

Mark continued as if she hadn't spoken, as if he hadn't noticed the emphasis on the word. Perhaps he hadn't. 'How's your dad now you've moved out?'

'He's OK... When I first left, he was calling twice a day to check where things are at home and stuff like that. He'd not be able to find a particular saucepan or something like that. He would phone to ask if I knew where it was. I think he's a bit lonely. I spoke to him a couple of days ago and he told me he'd taken up bowling.'

'Ten-pin?'

Poppy sniggered: 'On a lawn. I think some of the blokes in the village have started a club. I joked that he wouldn't be able to bend down to bowl the ball and he said it wasn't far from the truth.'

'What about you?'

'What about me?'

'How are you? New home, new job, new city. Lots of new stuff there.'

Poppy could feel the sun prickling her bare shoulders. It took her a while to reply, to choose the words carefully.

'It's awkward to meet new people,' Poppy said. 'People who aren't weirdoes.'

'How do you know if someone's a weirdo?'

'That's the point. You don't know, at first. One minute, you're happily sitting in a café and you start chatting to this girl who's reading a book you like. You swap smiles and hellos, ask if she wants anything from the counter… Next thing you know, she's asking if you're into sadomasochism.'

Mark almost fell off the wall as he burst into laughter. 'That happened to you?'

'Two days after I moved in! I've not been back to the café since.'

'Maybe that's the locals' way of welcoming you to the area?'

Poppy tucked a loose thread of hair behind her ear. Over in the beer garden opposite, some bloke in a vest was stacking plastic pint glasses into a flexible snake. Each time he added another, a cheer went up.

'Enough about me,' she said. 'How are you?'

'All right. Uni's going well. I've been getting into special effects.'

'Huh?'

'Like in movies and on TV – but smaller. It's all done on computers. It's not really my degree, but I started helping out one of the lads on my hallway who's doing film studies. Then we were playing FIFA with someone else from his course, and it turned out that this other lad's dad runs an independent production company. I'm going to do some work experience with him in a couple of weeks when he's back from holiday. I've joined the film club, too.'

'That sounds really exciting.'

'I suppose.' Mark's creeping smile gave away the fact that he thought it was much more than that. He was clearly thrilled about the work experience.

They sat quietly for a moment, listening to the alcohol-fuelled laughter from the beer garden.

From nowhere, Mark sighed, his chin dropped to his chest. 'I'm sorry, Pops.'

'For what?'

He shrugged, saying nothing for a few seconds. Poppy wondered if he meant the kiss. Was he sorry for it happening, or sorry that he'd not mentioned it since? It wasn't as if *she'd* brought it up, but still…

He didn't reply properly, leaving her to wonder. Eventually, he changed the subject. 'Did you read your mum's letter today?' he asked.

'Not yet.' Poppy patted Mark's arm, nodding towards Iris, who was returning from the pier.

He stood up quickly, leaning in closer to Poppy. 'Will you do something for me?'

'What?'

'Draw.'

My dearest Poppy,

So, this is it then? The end of the terrible teens. I hope you enjoyed these past seven years, because there's no going back. There are so many things about those times that you'll remember forever because they are the years that have shaped who you are to become.

As I was coming out of my teens, I'd just started to see your father: the mysterious – and easily manipulated! – Mr K. (We didn't call it 'dating' then). It was nothing too fancy – not our thing. We'd visit the coast to buy chips – there's nothing like seaside chips – or go to 'the pictures' as we used to call them. I'm not sure when or why people stopped. Sometimes, we'd simply go out for a drive. There were nowhere near as many cars on the roads back then and we had some great times turning the music up and driving aimlessly.

Not too long after the events in my last letter, your father had moved to the south-west. He was older than me, which meant the odd raised eyebrow, but it didn't affect either of us.

Very soon after, we decided to move in together. I know that sounds ridiculously quick – and it was – but it was also practical, for many boring reasons. In short, we were able to live in a much nicer place by pooling our money.

That's how and why I ended up moving back to Purley, this time with your father in tow. We bought the house in which we've lived ever since – but it was very different then, as you may have heard us say. It had been lived in by a retired couple with no children and had gone to ruin as they'd become too old to look after the place. We bought it at auction after they'd died and it was quite the wreck. Your father and I worked at our jobs through the week and then spent large parts of each weekend fixing and repairing. We went through that pattern for months and months.

And that's how your father nearly electrocuted himself!

He really won't appreciate me telling you this, but...

We were refitting the bathroom. We did a lot of the work ourselves. Things like tiling and grouting are easier than they look – although as boring as they sound. Your father was unscrewing the pulley cord that turned the lights on and off, when I asked him if he'd turned the electricity off. He said yes, so I asked him if he was sure. Your father turned to me with that slight frown of his – you'll know this look – and said, 'Of course I have,' as if I was an utter fool for thinking otherwise.

I shrugged and thought, 'Fair enough' – then watched as he jabbed a screwdriver into the live cable. Luckily, he was wearing rubber-soled shoes and gloves. Nevertheless, he fell off the chair and dislocated his shoulder.

We've never spoken of this since!

The reason I've included this is so that the next time he gives you that look – the one that makes you feel tiny and stupid – just remember that was the look he gave me just before he stuck a screwdriver into a live cable.

Anyway, back to when we'd first bought the house. Because I was living in the village, it seemed silly not to visit or talk to my mother. She was never a telephone person but had sent me a few cordial – if slightly distant – letters when I was living in Ledford. I'd visited her a few times but always by myself.

This was to be the first time she met my boyfriend – your father. It was a beautifully sunny day and she invited us in, then served us home-made lemonade, as well as strawberries and clotted cream. It was all very pleasant, very English, very her.

As the visit wore on I knew there was something wrong, though, because she was saying so little. Every time she spoke, it was a one-line answer and she made no effort to ask about your father, or our house. After a while of this, I couldn't help myself, so I asked what was wrong. Her head shot around to glare at me in a way I'd not seen in years. She was furious, staring daggers. She rose up, pointing a finger at the two of us, telling me we were 'living in sin'. She said I had embarrassed her in front of the village, that people were laughing at her.

Her eyes narrowed and she stepped closer to me, still pointing her finger as she said she'd never forgive me.

I do wonder why she invited us at all. She probably thought it was the only way she might get both of us there together.

I was so shocked that I snapped. All those years, all the tiny little digs, all the disappointed looks that she'd given me. I lost control. Suddenly I was standing, pointing and shouting. I'd never stood up to her like that before, but I told her I hated her.

I stormed out of the house and ran home, grabbed the keys and got into the car. I needed to be away from her, away from the village. Your father had followed me; he got into the passenger seat, trying to calm me down, but I wasn't listening.

I can't really describe it now because I've never been that angry before or since. I don't remember starting the car but I do remember driving out of the village. I was going so fast, so carelessly. The sun had gone, like the sky was matching my mood: it was grey and raining. I remember blinking and suddenly realising where I was and what I was doing. We were on these country roads with high hedges, tight turns and no pavements. There was this bend, but I saw it too late. I stamped on the brake and then…

I woke up in hospital three weeks later.

Pops, it's taken me a long time to write these past few paragraphs because I've spent so long trying to forget that day. It was the darkest thing I've ever done; my biggest secret, if you like. I know that, as you read this, you'll probably think less of me – and you really should. Trust me, you won't be able to think any worse of me than I still think of myself.

The car slammed into a tree. If you want to know why your father limps slightly, why he has problems with his lower back – that's the reason. It's not because of his age. He's been saying that ever since it happened. It's because of me. He could have died – we both could. After the accident, he had a small part of his spine removed and I was in a coma.

When I woke up, pretty much the first thing I remember was asking him if he was OK. When I knew he was, I remembered what I'd said to my mum. Those are the types of words you cannot take back.

I told your father I wanted to see my mum and he exchanged this quick look with the doctors.

And I knew.

Your father told me she'd had a heart attack shortly after the police officer had visited to tell her about the crash.

My greatest shame became double-fold. Not only did I nearly kill your father and myself, endangering everyone else on the road at the same time, I never had a chance to tell my mum that I was sorry for what I'd said.

As I've told you before, there was so much we'd never spoken of. It was only later, when I went through her papers, that I realised she'd been orphaned and evacuated because of the war.

Those are conversations that I might have had with her one day, if she'd lived.

It's not worth burning bridges, Poppy. You might be unhappy in a job and want to leave – but doing so in a huff and spouting what you believe to be home truths might come back to bite you. It'll feel good for a few hours and then, at a later date, you'll realise that you need that person's help or advice, or a reference from them, but you can't turn to them any longer. You might dislike a person and say something out of turn, then find out a short while later that they're dating your best friend.

I learned the hard way that sometimes it is better to say nothing.

I'm sorry that this is the way you had to find out about this part of my life. Perhaps it's something I should have told you about in person, while I still could – but it's not the easiest of things to bring up.

Either way, I love you, and I'm so sorry. Happy birthday.

Mum

Twenty-One

Freya was standing behind the only armchair in Poppy's flat, fingers tugging at Poppy's hair as she separated it into bundles.

'Come on, Pops,' Freya said. 'You can't spend your twenty-first in some boring gallery. You're twenty-one, not sixty-one.'

'I'm not *only* going to the gallery,' Poppy replied. 'Going out afterwards is fine. I'll be done by eight.'

'Yeah, but we could be in the pub at seven. If you're not getting there until, say, half-eight, that's way less time to get bladdered. The pubs close at midnight on Sundays.'

'Sorry.'

Freya braided together the three bunches on the right-hand side of Poppy's head, knitting them until she'd created the first pigtail. She moved over to the left-hand side, and waited until she had the second set of bunches pulled tightly before she dropped the slightly predictable bombshell.

'My rent's going to be a bit late this month,' she said. 'It's coming – promise this time. My mum's sending me money on PayPal, so I'll sort it out when it comes through. It'll be a day or two. Three at the most. Definitely no more than four.'

She pulled Poppy's head to the side as she completed the second pigtail and tied it at the bottom. When she was done, she flopped onto the nearby sofa that doubled as her bed.

Strictly speaking, Freya shouldn't have been living in Poppy's flat, given the whole 'no sub-letting' clause in the contract. Sod it, though, Poppy had thought when Freya had suggested it. Poppy needed the money in order to remain in the city. Freya had been late with rent for both months she'd been living there but she always paid in the end.

Freya picked up a celebrity magazine from the floor and started to flick through it. Poppy wasn't sure where it had come from, considering that she hadn't bought it and that Freya supposedly had no money, but she didn't ask.

'How's the job hunting?' Poppy asked.

Freya didn't look up. 'I'm either under- or overqualified. Just cos I got a third for my degree, most companies hiring graduates don't want me; then, because I have a degree, all these other bosses reckon I'll show them up by being so smart. I can't win, Pops.'

Poppy decided not to point out the fact that Freya had only started looking for jobs in the past few weeks, rather than during her final year at university as many other students would have done.

'It's not my fault,' Freya added, even though Poppy hadn't spoken. 'Mark was always the one with the books and all that. I can't do exams. I'm like… What's it called?' She clicked her fingers in Poppy's direction. 'Dyslexic. Yeah, I'm dyslexic. They didn't take that into account when they did the marking. It's, like, prejudice and all that.'

Poppy had known Freya for fifteen years and this was the first time she'd ever heard of any potential dyslexia. Something else she didn't point out.

Freya dropped the magazine to the floor and started filing her nails with such ferocity that there was a danger she might start a fire. 'Can you believe Mark's engaged?' she said.

'Well—'

'I wouldn't put it past him to have done it just to get at me. Make me jealous, y'know?'

Poppy stared at her, mouth slightly open. 'You broke up with him two and a half years ago!'

'Yeah, but you should've heard him, Pops. He was texting, calling, Facebook messaging. He wanted to get back with me. I always thought we'd end up hooking up again after uni – but then he went out and found this Iris girl. I thought it'd be a quick Manchester thing, then he gets engaged. It's ridiculous.'

'I suppose they are a bit young…'

Freya almost leapt off the sofa, arms flailing: 'Exactly! Then he's always online, going on about some job he's got working on films and that. He was always a geek. Can you believe it?'

'I think it's something to do with the dad of one of his friends. He—'

'Oh, so it's not *what* you know, it's *who* you know. The funny handshake brigade and all that. All right for some.'

'I don't think—'

But Freya was on a roll. 'So not only has he got some dodgy job, he's then jumped into some engagement. She must've pushed him into it. Maybe he's having a breakdown or something? I keep thinking I should go up there and talk some sense into him.' Freya stared at Poppy, looking for support that hadn't been coming the first time she'd suggested it, let alone now they were onto the seventh or eighth.

'I don't think that's a good idea,' Poppy said.

'Why not?'

'Because he sounds fine every time I talk to him. They're getting married next summer…'

'Pah! If it lasts that long. I give it three months, tops. Christmas at the latest. Have you heard from him recently?'

Poppy picked up the tin of coloured pencils from the table and put them into her knapsack. 'Not really. Look, I've got to go, Frey. Thanks for doing my hair.' She stood, lifted the bag onto her shoulders, then crouched and kissed her friend on the forehead. 'I'll see you in the Red Griffin later, OK? Like I said, I'm leaving the gallery at eight, so I'll see you a bit after that.'

Freya scooped her magazine up from the floor and crossed her knees defensively. 'I'm not being a bitch, Pops. I really think he might have had a breakdown. He's not replying to my texts; you say you've not heard from him. What if she's blackmailing him, or something?'

Poppy stood in the doorway, key in her hand. 'She's not blackmailing him – and I *really* have to go. We can talk more later, all right?'

She didn't wait for the reply before pulling the door closed and heading for the stairs.

Even though it was Sunday, the pavements of Bristol were buzzing with early evening excitement. There must have been some sort of sporting event going on because groups of men were swarming around the open paved areas, singing and celebrating. In some places this might have had an edge but the atmosphere was pleasant. The men stepped aside to make way for a family on their way to or from Sunday dinner.

Poppy passed the independent bakery where she occasionally treated herself to an almond croissant, and continued across College Green, past the cathedral, until she reached the large glass doors of the Parkway Gallery. It was an impressive building, despite its smallish size. It might have once had two floors but now there was only one, with a high, echoing ceiling atop a wooden floor polished to perfection. Flawless white walls surrounded the space, with a smattering of paintings pinned evenly along them. Two inverted triangle sculptures stood in the furthest corner: one jet-black, the other a beaming white.

In the centre of the floor were two rows of chairs facing one another, each with an easel and canvas before them. Against one of the walls there was a long table, on which stood a large tea urn and piles of glistening china cups. Poppy placed her bag on one of the chairs and then helped herself to a cup of tea before joining the half-dozen people chatting at the back of the room.

She was often running late for class, arriving in a gust of air and full of apologies. Today, for once, she was early – solely because she couldn't stand listening to Freya going on about Mark any longer. It wasn't *becoming* an obsession; it *was* an obsession. It had got to the stage where Freya would rather believe her ex-boyfriend had gone through a breakdown than accept that he was in love with someone else.

As Poppy approached, a man opened his arms to welcome her. He was wearing a brown cord jacket with olive green elbow patches, matching trousers and a flowery shirt with a frilly collar.

'Poppy, my love,' he called, air-kissing beside her cheek and then shaking her hand for good measure. 'It's so wonderful to see you again.'

'Good to see you, too, Derek,' she replied.

'Are you all set for tonight?'

'I think so.'

'Oooh, I *know* so. What is your everyday life object?'

Poppy led him back to her bag, where she pulled out a tin full of coloured pencils. Some had been worn down to a tiny, blunt stump, others were longer and sharper.

Derek seemed confused. 'These are your *tools* – but what everyday object will you be drawing?'

Poppy took out a second tin of pencils, these ones brand new. 'I got these today. I'm going to use the new ones to draw the old ones.'

A grin spread across Derek's face. 'Oh, that's very smart, my girl. Out with the old, in with the new. The circle of life for an artist. And, of course, the pencils are an everyday object for you. Very clever indeed. I can't wait to see what you come up with.' He placed a fatherly hand on her shoulder and Poppy shrank under his praise, having not actually thought of the meaning he'd suggested. Not knowingly, anyway. She'd thought the pencil tin would be a fun thing to draw.

'I suppose we should start,' Derek added, before clapping his hands together.

The half-dozen people at the back joined a few late stragglers on the chairs, with each laying out the object they'd brought. Someone was arranging a pair of scuffed trainers to draw; someone else had a set of cutlery.

Poppy arranged her well-used pencils on a small tea table in front of her and then made sure she was comfortable at the easel before starting to draw.

Poppy had largely kept to the promise she had made Mark the year before, to work on her art. Purley had been so familiar that she'd struggled to find anything that inspired her, but in Bristol, there were new things to see everywhere. Sometimes she drew pictures of pictures, copying the graffiti that adorned various buildings. Other times, she focused on people, or on things like the quirky independent shops that lined the back streets. There was no particular subject she enjoyed more than any other, but the more she drew, the more she noticed the little things around the city.

After a while, Derek came and stood by Poppy's shoulder, watching her pencil strokes. He said nothing at first, but she could tell from the way he was bouncing on his heels that he was happy with her.

He eventually crouched down to her level. 'Confidence,' he whispered, quietly enough that only Poppy could hear.

'Pardon?' she replied, not stopping what she was doing.

'It's about confidence, my girl. When you question yourself, that self-doubt shows in your stroke marks.' He wafted a hand towards the canvas. '*This* is confidence, pure and simple. Do you understand what I've been trying to tell you now?'

Poppy scraped the lead harshly across the surface, hatching a small shadow underneath her well-worn blue pencil. 'Yes,' she replied, meaning it. When Derek had first got on to her about being more confident in her art, she had wanted to tell him to get lost. She'd thought he was some eccentric old nutter.

It had taken her a while to take on board what he was trying to say. In the end, she'd gained confidence not because he'd told her she needed it, but because he'd talked her through the good things she was doing. Positivity bred positivity and, before long, she hadn't needed him to tell her what she was doing right. She knew it, instinctively.

He was still eccentric, though.

'Are we still on for later?' he asked as he stood.

Poppy looked up at him. 'If you still want to.'

He winked as he pirouetted around her chair. 'Oh, I wouldn't miss it for the world, darling.'

When class was over, Poppy stopped for a quick chat with some of the others, wolfed down a couple of sandwiches from her bag in the hope the bread would help keep the upcoming alcohol at bay, and then headed back through the glass doors.

She was at a pelican crossing, waiting to cross the road, when a familiar voice called her name. Poppy turned at the same time as the green man started beeping and flashing, which left her with one foot in the road, one on the pavement.

'Dad?'

Poppy's father was hurrying towards her, looking far more dishevelled than usual. There were sweat stains under the armpits of his white shirt, and he'd unfastened the top two buttons, allowing a wiry Brillo pad of hair to escape. He was wearing shorts, too – the type that had been tailored in order to look smart, but only ever looked ridiculous. If a man was going to wear shorts, it should be all or nothing: casual and loose, never turn-ups with a belt buckle.

She realised, as he reached her, that he didn't look like *her* dad, he looked like *a* dad. After all these years, he'd finally found that old person's clothes shop, where they stocked garments no one under the age of fifty would even attempt to pull off.

'I thought I'd missed you,' he said, hands on his hips, trying to catch his breath. 'I've been running but I went the wrong way, then I asked for directions but I think I misheard the guy. I ended up going all the way up this massive hill, then I realised that was the wrong direction, too, so had to come down again.' He wheezed a huge gulp of oxygen and then tried to stand up straight. Although he couldn't quite manage it, he passed over a card-shaped envelope. 'Happy birthday.'

Poppy took it. She was staring at her father as he leaned against a wall, fighting to catch his breath. She'd spoken to him regularly, but hadn't seen him in a couple of months – save for a few snatched moments on Skype in which he'd failed to readjust the camera from giving her an up-nostril shot.

'Let's have a sit-down,' Poppy said mercifully, leading her dad towards a pair of benches close to the cathedral. It was a little after eight and there were far fewer people around than before Poppy's class had started. A few die-hard drinkers were swigging from cans of extra-strength lager close to College Green, while a small group of lads with skateboards were practising tricks on a nearby paved area. Their wheels scraped and skidded across the ground, but otherwise it was quiet.

'You should've said you were coming,' Poppy said, handing her father a bottle of water from her bag.

He gulped down a few mouthfuls and, as he leaned back on the bench, finally caught his breath. 'It was a last-minute thing,' he said, flexing his legs. 'Sorry, Pops, I'm going to have to keep walking, else my knees will cramp up.'

Poppy pointed to the area behind them. 'Queen Square is over the bridge. It's really pretty. We can go for a walk there.'

'Sounds good.'

Poppy helped her father up and then they walked slowly in the direction she'd indicated.

'I was sitting at home watching television, but thinking about how it was your twenty-first,' her dad said. 'Then I thought I could come and see you. You're only up the road, really, aren't you? I thought it'd be a surprise. I hadn't thought about the fact that you might be out. When I got to your house, Freya said you were at the gallery and that you all had plans for later. She was very clear that you had plans! I'd already paid for parking and walked to your flat, so didn't want to move the car again. I started walking towards the centre, then time was getting on, so I started running.'

Poppy didn't want to say anything, but to her, he sounded lost in more than a geographic sense. It didn't seem natural for him to have made such a series of poor decisions. She linked her arm through his and moved closer, even though he was still sweating in the late evening warmth.

'Aww, Dad…'

'I'm sorry, I—'

'Don't be sorry – it's great to see you. I wish you'd said you were coming. We could've gone out for something to eat.'

'I know, I know…' He nodded at the envelope still in her hand. 'It's just some money. I didn't know what to get you and thought that this way, you can do what you want with it.'

Poppy clasped the envelope tighter but laughed. 'I made that exact argument when I was fourteen and you told me, "No way."'

Her father turned and grinned. He finally seemed like the dad she used to know, his eyes full of authoritative mischief. There were crinkles around his mouth. 'Never question your father, Pops.'

They reached the square and started on a lap of the green. The smell of barbecue was floating on the air as a group of young people sat cross-legged on the grass with a pair of tin-foil disposable grills simmering away.

'I did have another reason for coming,' her dad added, turning away, smile disappearing.

'OK…'

'I didn't want to spoil your birthday, but we've both been so busy and I didn't want to tell you on the phone. And I can't get the computer thing to work.'

'Tell me what?'

'It's, um… Well… I don't know. It's sort of, erm… I was…'

'Just tell me, Dad.'

'I'm seeing someone.' He spoke so quickly that Poppy needed a couple of seconds to replay what he'd said. He must have mistaken her silence for disapproval, because he quickly followed up with: 'I would have told you sooner, but—'

'It's fine, Dad.'

He stopped what he had been saying and coughed slightly. 'Oh… You don't mind?'

'Why would I mind? It's been six years. I'd rather you were happy with someone than at home by yourself.'

He coughed again. 'I thought you might be upset?'

'Surely you know me better than that?'

Poppy's father started to say something and then stopped himself again, scratching his chin at the same time. 'You're right, I'm sorry. Her name's Madeleine. We were hoping you could come over for tea one Sunday, so you could meet each other.'

'That depends on what's going to be for tea.'

'Oh, um…'

Poppy nudged him with her elbow and laughed. 'I'm joking, Dad.' She turned to look at him as they walked side by side. 'Are you sure you're all right?'

He was still scratching, but closer to his ear this time. 'I've been worried about how you'd take things, then it was all a bit of a hurry when I decided to drive here.'

Poppy gripped his arm and pulled herself tight to him. 'Oh, Dad, you've got yourself into a right tizz. Everything's fine, OK? When I'm home tomorrow, I'll check my calendar and I'll call. We'll sort out a Sunday where you, Madeleine and I are all free. Either I can come to your house, or we'll go out somewhere. It'll be nice.'

Poppy's father perked up at this, losing the strange nervousness that she'd rarely seen before. He began to talk about how he'd been offered early retirement at work. He was seriously thinking about it, although he wasn't sure what he'd do with his time if he did so. Poppy let him speak, only replying when she had to, enjoying hearing him more relaxed.

Soon they were back where they'd started and recrossed the bridge, heading towards College Green. Poppy's father wasn't completely sure where he'd left the car, but he knew it was on the way back to her flat, so Poppy walked him there. After a hug goodbye, he got into the car and then almost headed the wrong way down a one-way street before catching himself and following the signs. Poppy watched him disappear around a bend and then checked her phone. It was nine o'clock – and she was late for her own party.

Poppy was only halfway through the double doors of the Red Griffin when a voice bellowed, 'Pops!' Freya was wedged into a corner booth with four pint glasses spread around the table in front of her.

'Thank God you're here,' Freya said, standing and nodding at the glasses. 'I was trying to make it look like there was a group of us so nobody nicked the table. I've been dying for a wee.'

She pushed past Poppy and ran towards the ladies' toilets, shouting, 'Coming through!' as she shouldered past two old men having a quiet pint. Poppy noticed that the four glasses were all almost empty. She dropped her jacket on the circular sofa surrounding the table and then spotted a couple of her office colleagues close to the bar. They didn't know Freya – and Freya wouldn't have known them. They'd all been waiting for the birthday girl.

Poppy waved them over, then saw three more huddled near a fruit machine on the far side of the bar. By the time Freya returned from the toilet, Poppy's party was in full swing, with eight of her work friends present, plus Freya. Poppy thanked everyone for coming and then got to work on the cocktails everyone was offering to buy her.

As the evening went on, Poppy didn't exactly go out of her way to avoid Freya, but she ended up in conversation with a couple of her workmates nevertheless. Freya was on the other end of the sofa, sipping her fifth pint of the evening. On a couple of occasions, one of the other guests had joined Freya and tried to start a conversation, but she'd been feverishly tapping away on her phone every few minutes, which had put an end to any interest.

At a few minutes to ten, the doors were flung open in true Wild West style, revealing Derek in bright red trousers and jacket. He was wearing the same flowery shirt as earlier. He skipped into the pub, making a beeline for Poppy – seemingly far more excited than she was.

'Here's the birthday girl,' he cooed and, for a moment, she thought he was going to pinch her cheeks. Luckily, he didn't. Instead he waved towards the barman, whom he apparently knew, and asked for a G&T.

'I didn't know you came in here,' Poppy said.

'Oh, I know *all* the bar-folk round here.' Derek offered Poppy a wicked grin and then insisted on being introduced to all her friends. He air-kissed a couple, shook hands with the less sure, and then settled on Freya. 'I *love* your hair,' he said.

Freya had puffed her hair into a ball with tails at the back. She frowned at him. 'Er, thanks.'

Poppy introduced them to one another and there was an awkward handshake that was enthusiastic from Derek's end, less so from

Freya's. As if suddenly realising there were other people around, Freya tucked her phone into her bra and downed the rest of her pint.

'You dancing, birthday girl?' she asked, turning to Poppy and ignoring Derek.

Poppy shook her head. 'Not yet; I'm still talking to people. In a bit.'

Freya frowned again and then gave a 'suit yourself' shrug before heading towards the small wooden-floored area close to the toilets. At a massive push, it could be described as a dance floor, but it could probably hold a maximum of four people if no one moved very much. As it was, Freya had the space to herself.

'She's an… *interesting* character,' Derek said, as they watched her.

'Flatmate,' Poppy said.

Freya was in her own world, dancing to Nirvana while the speakers pumped out Michael Bolton. Her hair flailed as she headbanged through a chorus nobody else could hear.

'*Flatmate?*' Derek repeated.

'We've known each other a long time,' Poppy said.

'I hope you don't take this the wrong way, but I wouldn't have pegged you as friends.'

Poppy turned to him, taking in the red trousers, red jacket and frilly, flowery shirt. 'People could say the same about the two of us.'

Derek was about to sip from his gin and tonic, but he nearly dropped it as he burst into a guffaw of laughter. 'Oh, my dear girl, you're absolutely right. How utterly awful of me.' He grinned wider. 'I'm such a bitch.'

'You're right, though,' Poppy said. 'We've gone in different directions since we were kids. Freya tells me she's not got enough money to pay her part of the rent, but she's gone through at least six pints since about eight o'clock. Maybe more.'

A pause. Derek raised his eyebrows. 'Are you saying she has a drinking problem?'

Poppy said nothing, continuing to stare at Freya, who was twerking with a radiator pipe.

'Good point,' Derek added.

He turned to the side, leaning in a little closer. When he next spoke, much of the flamboyance had gone from his voice. 'I don't mean to patronise, but there is a difference between someone who *likes* to drink, and someone with a drinking *problem*. As much as it pains me to say this, that is especially true with young people who are able to push their limits far further than someone of my, ahem, *experience*.' A small grin. 'I'm not saying you're wrong, nor trying to change your mind on anything – you know her far better than me – I'm simply saying that not everything is a *problem* as such.'

Poppy nodded. 'I don't know if it's a problem – it's not like she drinks every night – she's just a bad drunk. Does that make sense?'

'Perfectly.'

As Freya flipped her hair, her gaze swept across Poppy and Derek from the far side of the bar. Even from that distance, Poppy saw her friend's eyes narrow as she realised they were watching her. She stopped dancing and stomped towards them. Sweat was pouring from her forehead, running around her eyes and dribbling down her cheeks. Her skirt had hitched itself up, revealing the upper part of her thighs. She glanced between Derek and Poppy, then settled on the birthday girl. 'You dancing yet?'

'In a bit, Frey.'

'How about another drink?'

Poppy pointed at the three multicoloured cocktails on the table next to her. 'I think I'm all right for most of the night.'

Freya threw both arms up in annoyance. 'You can down those three and get more in. It's your twenty-first; you should be going crazy.'

Poppy shook her head. 'I'm not really in the mood. I'm happy having a few quieter drinks.'

'Oh, like that, is it? "Quieter" as in, "Without Freya"? First Mark, now you.'

Poppy had to hold back a sigh. If she'd had much more to drink then her tongue might have been looser. She'd been trying, *really* trying, to take her mother's advice from the previous year.

'Not *without* you,' she said. 'I love it that you're here – and I'm happy for people to do their own thing. If you want to dance, that's fine. I want to talk for the moment.'

Freya had one hand on her hip, head at an angle as she stared at Poppy. 'You're taking Mark's side, aren't you?'

Poppy's mouth was open, tongue on her bottom row of teeth. She was unsure what to say. 'I'm not sure what you mean by sides,' she said. 'He's marrying another girl. What do you want me to say?'

'I want you to say *something* to him.'

'About what? You broke up with him two and a half years ago! You did that and he moved on.' She reached out to touch Freya's shoulder in a conciliatory gesture, but Poppy had misjudged quite how angry her friend was. Freya slapped the hand away, with a vicious crack that echoed around the rapidly silencing room.

Poppy pulled away, not hurt by the blow, more shocked by the noise and Freya's aggression. Derek stepped forward, putting himself between the two girls. 'Now, come on,' he said sternly.

Freya's eyes were slits, staring furiously at him. 'Who are you? I've known her since we were six. Six! I know your sort – I've seen 'em at uni – pervy old men leering at young girls.' She flapped a hand towards Poppy. 'She's twenty-one, you creepy old bastard. You should be ashamed of yourself.'

Silence.

Pint glasses were hovering in mid-air between table and mouth; jaws had dropped; eyes were boggling. Even the music had stopped.

Poppy stepped back in front of Derek, pushing herself onto her tiptoes. 'Say you're sorry,' she said, eyeball to eyeball with Freya.

'I'm *not* sorry; I'm saving you from a pervert.' She spat the final word over Poppy's shoulder.

'You're not saving me from anyone.'

'I am, he's—'

'He's gay.'

'—just a filthy old—' Freya stopped herself, mouth hanging open. 'He's *gay*?'

'Didn't the bright red trousers give it away?' Poppy turned to Derek, holding out a hand to indicate his clothes. 'Sorry, Derek, but, y'know…'

Derek smoothed down his blazer. Poppy hadn't known him that long, but she knew him well enough to see he was fighting back a smile. 'No offence taken; not from you, anyway. And I'll have you know, I happen to *like* these trousers.' He finally broke, and the grin spread across his face. He raised his voice. 'All right, move along, chop chop. Nothing to see here.'

The crowd slowly returned their attentions to their drinks.

Poppy turned back to Freya. 'Say you're sorry.' The sternness of her voice surprised even her. She sounded like a grown-up.

Freya stared defiantly into Poppy's eyes. She wasn't usually one for giving ground, let alone admitting she'd made a mistake. For a second, Poppy thought she was going to storm away but, eventually, Freya took a small step backwards and turned to Derek. 'Sorry, man, it's er… Well, y'know how it is…'

It was as good as he was going to get and Derek knew it. He reached out his hand and shook Freya's. 'No offence taken,' he said.

'I think we should probably go back to the flat,' Poppy said, putting a hand on Freya's shoulder and not having it slapped away this time.

'It's your birthday, Pops.'

'And I'm more than happy spending it with you. C'mon…'

Poppy said some quick, apologetic goodbyes to her workmates. They'd all seen what had happened and none of them queried her decision to leave. She collected their things, and then took Freya's arm and led her onto the street. Freya was dragging her feet, peering back over her shoulder towards the pub. A bouncer had appeared on the door.

'You all right, ladies?' he asked.

'Piss off,' Freya spat back.

Poppy directed her along the street and across the road, before they headed into an alley that provided a shortcut to their flat. When they were eclipsed by the darkness of the surrounding buildings, Freya shook off Poppy's hand and reached into her bag for a cigarette. She leaned against the wall and lit it, taking a deep drag.

'Want one?' she asked.

'Not today.'

Freya didn't hold back, taking an even deeper puff second time around. 'I was trying to help,' she said, hostility returning to her voice.

'I know you were, but those are my friends.'

'*I'm* your friend. Your *best* friend. We've always been best friends.'

This time, Poppy couldn't stop the sigh from escaping.

'What?' Freya said.

'Nothing.'

'No, go on, say it. You're obviously thinking it.'

Poppy rolled her eyes, not wanting an argument but seemingly in line for one anyway. 'You broke up with Mark, Frey. *You*. It's over. You have to let it go and move on. The drinking; the aggression. You let it mess up your final year at uni and now you have to figure out what to do. You're not getting back together. He's marrying somebody else.'

Freya tossed the still-lit cigarette to the ground and watched it smoulder, the orange embers fizzing in the darkness. Her fists were clenched, shoulders tense. Poppy had known her for most of their lives but had no idea what she was going to do next.

Which was why it was such a surprise when Freya slumped forward, tears streaming down her face, hands covering her eyes. 'Oh, Pops…'

Freya bawled a string of garbled apologies onto Poppy's shoulder. The only word Poppy caught clearly was 'Mark'. She smoothed her friend's hair, holding her close, feeling the tears on her bare skin.

'Happy birthday,' she whispered, quietly enough that not even Freya could hear.

My dearest Poppy,

I suspect you've probably had enough of the boring lessons and lectures from me by now. It's your twenty-first birthday, so I thought I'd tell you the story of something I'm surprised you never asked about.

Your name.

I realise I'm zipping forward in time a little bit but I figured you deserved something special for such a monumental birthday.

Your father and I didn't know ahead of time that we were going to have a girl. I suppose we were a tiny bit old-fashioned in the sense that we wanted it to be a surprise. You arrived late – a story I'll come to – which led your father to decree on the day you were due that you had to be a girl. I jokingly called him a sexist and then, unfortunately, he turned out to be correct. You let me down!

Anyway, we bought a giant book of children's names. Separately from one another, we compiled top-ten lists of what we might want to call you.

The aim was that, within our respective tens, we'd have at least one name on which we'd agree.

Perhaps predictably, there was not a single name on my list that matched your father's. My number one choice was 'Eleanor' (I can't remember why), while your father liked the name 'Beatrice'.

He looked through my ten while I went through his. Neither of us were convinced by the other's choices – which left us calling you 'the baby'. Your father had a few other names for you considering the hours at which you woke us up in those early days, but let's not get into those.

Some time had passed since we got you home and it was getting to the point where we had to file the birth certificate. Things had dragged on to such a degree that nothing was off the table. It was probably the exhaustion but I'd hear random words on TV or the radio, like 'Star' or 'Meadow', for instance, and I'd find myself wondering if that was a good name.

Actually, it was definitely the exhaustion. 'Star' would have been a dreadful choice.

I'd find myself justifying such awful suggestions. Your father would stare at me and say something like, 'You want to call her,

"Genesis"?', and I'd reply with things like, 'Well, it is different. It is a new beginning, after all.'

Anyway, my old friend Sharon drove down from Birmingham to see you. She was also married at this point, though the less said about that, the better.

Life had got in the way and we hadn't seen each other in the best part of a year. I was pregnant and travelling wasn't so comfortable but, in truth, we'd been drifting apart for a while anyway. In the sixteen years since, we've probably only seen each other six or seven times, and always spend most of our time reminiscing over those old days.

I digress.

Sharon was suggesting even worse names than the ones I'd come up with. Her main idea was, of course, 'Sharon'. 'It's a good name,' she assured me. 'You can't go wrong with it.'

After I dismissed that, she said she'd always liked the name 'Moon'. I have no idea what came over me, but if it wasn't for your father's voice of reason, that would have probably been your name.

In the time since we'd got you home, we'd received a good couple of dozen 'congratulations' cards. Sharon was going through them, figuring out how many of our old friends had got in contact. Most of the cards had the usual type of pictures. A pink elephant; a pink penguin; a baby in a pink crib; a couple that simply said the word 'baby' on the front. In pink lettering, of course.

Among everything was a card completely different to the others. It had come from Mr Ashcroft across the road and, if I'm honest, I suspect it was one he'd had lying around in a box for years. There were no words on the inside and it was likely one of those blank ones that can be purposed for any occasion.

The front was a print of a painting showing a cream vase filled with red flowers. Sharon asked why someone had sent us a card with tulips on the front – and your father replied that they were poppies painted by Van Gogh.

It was one of those strange moments that are hard to explain after the event. As if a light bulb had gone on. Your father looked to me and I looked at him and we knew that was your name.

I hope you like it and that it's working out well for you. At least we didn't go for 'Vincent'.

You may or may not remember – but when you were old enough to start naming things, you called your first doll 'Nissan' after next door's car. I think we did a better job than that.

Happy birthday,

Mum

Twenty-Two

Poppy might have been unsure at first but she now knew Whitby was most definitely a seaside resort. She also knew it took a bloody long time to reach the north-east town when setting off from the south-west of England.

Her back was aching from the trio of train journeys, pair of bus trips and taxi ride. It had been almost nine hours of travelling.

The solid wooden bench on which she was sitting wasn't helping, either.

Poppy wriggled, trying to get comfortable, and then stopped as Mark caught her eye over Iris's shoulder. She couldn't be sure but thought he might have winked at her. The glint in his eye almost made her laugh but, as quickly as his attention had been on her, it was gone again as he focused back on the vicar.

It was the first time Poppy had seen Mark in person – been close enough to touch him – since the trip she'd taken to Blackpool two years before. Every so often, they had messaged back and forth about meeting somewhere between Manchester and Bristol for a meal and a catch-up, but it hadn't happened. Either she'd had work or something had come up with her father or Freya. If not that, then Mark had been busy with his work, Iris, or the general wedding planning.

There was always something.

The frequency of the texts and instant messages had started to fizzle out and Poppy had wondered if she'd even end up attending the wedding to which she'd been invited. But she was here, of course. Nervous on Mark's behalf, not to mention her own. She'd wondered if their old spark of friendship would still be there but all it had taken was that one look – the possible wink, the half-smile – and she'd known. Of course it was still there.

'Then it's time for the second reading,' the vicar said solemnly.

Poppy had never been to a wedding rehearsal before – she hadn't even been to a wedding in about a decade. As far as she could tell, the rehearsal was essentially the same as the wedding itself but no one had to dress up, there was less faffing in general, and no binding vows at the end.

The wedding venue had taken Poppy's breath away when she'd first seen it. She'd climbed out of the taxi, her bag hefted on her shoulder, and then had to double check they were in the right place. The picturesque church was like something out of a postcard or a British rom-com. There was a pretty steeple attached to an old stone building, surrounded by acres of beautiful green. If that wasn't enough, it was on a hill high enough to be able to see the port and sea in the distance.

Poppy had arrived with minutes to spare and had left her bag at the back of the church before finding her spot on the pews. She'd not had a chance to talk to Mark, as he was at the front with his wife-to-be, but he and Iris had both seen her and offered small waves.

Both sides of the church were lined with rows of uncushioned wooden benches. The one for Iris's family and friends was packed front to back. Mark's side had Poppy, plus a dozen or so other people on the front two benches, with only a smattering of others behind.

Poppy had assumed it was key people only for the rehearsal – but someone on Iris's side obviously thought differently. Poppy was sitting behind Mark's mum and dad but, aside from them, she didn't know anyone. Considering Mark had lived there for eighteen years, Purley wasn't very well represented, she thought. Freya was a notable, if entirely understandable, absentee.

The vicar was wearing plain black trousers, a shirt with rolled-up sleeves, and a dog collar. Mark was in jeans and Iris in a long, floaty, tie-dyed skirt similar to the one Poppy had first seen her wearing. Everyone was dressed down and relaxed, except for the pair in the centre of the front row on Iris's side of the church.

Iris's mother was in a soft pink suit jacket with matching skirt and heels. Her husband was at her side, squirming uncomfortably in a full suit and tie. Poppy found herself watching them instead of Mark and Iris, fascinated by the dynamic between the older couple. Every time Iris's father fidgeted, his wife would hiss something and he'd sit up straighter. She was sitting tall, knees crossed, back straight, chin high, eyes fixed on her daughter and soon-to-be son-in-law.

A young woman climbed down from the pulpit, her reading done. She scuttled back to her seat with a small nod towards Iris.

The vicar thanked her and then continued. 'When the second reading's done, it's time for the serious stuff.' He grinned. 'I'll yammer on for a bit and I'll turn to you and say, "Do you take Iris Lacey Payne to be your lawfully wedded wife?"'

He nodded towards Mark, who was trying to keep a straight face as he held Iris's hand. 'Do I take who?' he joked. '*Iris?!*'

She slapped his arm and there was a tittering from the back of the church. Poppy noticed that Iris's mother didn't flinch, her smile that definitely *wasn't* a smile fixed in place.

'I hope you're going to remember her name tomorrow,' the vicar replied with a matey grin.

'I think I'll manage it.'

'Shall we go again?' The vicar asked. 'I'll say, "Do you take Iris Lacey Payne to be your lawfully wedded wife?" – and you'll say…'

'I do.'

'Good! Then I'll turn to you, Iris…'

The rehearsal continued in the same vein, with the vicar joining in with the laid-back atmosphere, and Iris asking one of the ushers if he'd step up if Mark forgot his lines. With things already jovial, the organist nearly brought the house down when, instead of playing Mendelssohn's 'Wedding March' at the end, she launched into an impressive rendition of Stealers Wheel's 'Stuck In The Middle With You'. As people cottoned on to what was happening, they laughed and hummed, with even the ones who didn't know the song clapping along, slightly oblivious to it all.

That was, except for Iris's mother, who was glaring angrily at anyone unlucky enough to catch her eye. Poppy stopped watching her, instead focusing on the hopefully happy couple as they trundled along the aisle, arm in arm. Mark smiled towards Poppy and definitely winked this time – before pinching his almost-wife's backside and getting a smacked wrist for his troubles.

Poppy still hadn't had a chance to get to her hotel. She was sitting in a beer garden, bag at her side. The pub itself was empty but the grass outside was covered with sunbathing drinkers enjoying the weather. Poppy wasn't sure how she'd managed it but, as she'd stumbled through the garden gate, an empty deckchair had appeared like a mirage. Before anyone could call dibs, she'd thrown herself into it.

'I'm not moving,' she said, as Mark approached with two bottles of pear cider.

He sat at her feet and passed her one of the bottles. 'Thanks for coming up. I know it's a long way.'

'It's not only a long way, it's a *really* long way. Do you know I could've flown to LA in the time it took me to get here?'

'Could you really?'

'Probably. Either way, I hope you appreciate it.'

Mark rested his head on the side of her chair. 'I really do, Pops. So does Iris.'

'You looked like you were having fun at the rehearsal.'

'It was her idea,' Mark said.

'Come off it. How long have I known you? The messing around was definitely *your* idea.'

He laughed. 'OK – it was *my* idea and she went along with it because she thought it'd be funny, too. Her mum had a bit of a fit afterwards and Iris took the blame. They've gone off to the hotel for the night now. Tomorrow's going to be all ties and top hats, so I thought that having a bit of fun today would get everyone in a lighter mood. The vicar was loving it. He told us he normally finds these things a bit boring. Did you hear the organist at the end? She told us she can do "Highway To Hell", too.'

'Don't churches draw the line at that?'

'AC/DC?'

She stared at him. 'Songs about hell, you div.'

He laughed. 'Right… Sorry. My brain's a bit mangled. This time tomorrow, I'm going to be married.'

'I did wonder why I'd come all this way.' Poppy had a sip of her drink and gave the customary gasp of enjoyment. 'I needed that.' She nodded at the group of people huddling close to a table. 'Talk me through who everyone is, then.'

Iris's father stood out in his suit, even though he had removed his jacket and tie. He seemed relieved to be away from the church, or possibly his wife, and was laughing away with a pint of ale in his hand. Mark's dad was there, too, thankfully not wearing the green dressing gown he'd had on the last time Poppy had seen him. Other than that, there were some of Mark's workmates, a few of Iris's male friends, people they knew from university, and Mark's best man.

'Your best man is Iris's brother?' Poppy queried, after he'd told her.

'It sort of happened by default,' Mark said. 'You know I never had many male friends in Purley – and that continued through uni. I could've asked Dad, I suppose, but he's a bit frail now and gets nervous around big organised events. Iris suggested her brother, and it seemed fair enough. His name's Liam. We've been out a few times and he's sound.'

'Not like the new mother-in-law, then…?'

Mark was saved from responding by Liam calling him over for pictures to be taken. There wasn't only a single wedding photographer, there were four: three carrying different-sized cameras, the other with a video camera and tripod. Poppy watched from afar as Mark was tugged and shunted into various poses, before the media crew took him off to a second patch of grass for yet more pictures. She'd never heard of wedding photographers getting involved the day *before*.

Poppy finished her cider and then fished through her bag. It had been a long, stressful day and, despite the hours of inertia, there was one thing she'd forgotten to do.

My dearest Poppy,

I suppose now I've given you the story of how I met your father and then nearly killed him, I should tell you about our wedding. If you're expecting some golden story, then I'm sorry to disappoint you. It was a very low-key day, very normal. My parents had died and your father's parents were both pensioners and didn't particularly want to be involved.

I'll cut through the organisational stuff, but, in short: it was a sunny day, we were on time, the Purley Church vicar was terrific, the speeches went well afterwards, and we all had a lovely time.

Nobody wants to hear that story, though, because straightforward weddings are boring. We want drunken bridesmaids falling over, best men forgetting their speeches and passing out, food fights, people objecting, and everything else.

In that respect, our wedding day is only half the story of our wedding.

My mother didn't travel and I was never brought up in a family for whom extravagant holidays were the norm. I'm not complaining about that, merely pointing out the truth. Largely because of that, though, I wanted to do something completely different for our honeymoon. We saved and saved, eventually settling on a two-week break to Barbados. I'd seen the photos in the brochures of those white-sand beaches and lovely turquoise ocean, and it seemed like such a change from anything I'd ever seen.

We were at Heathrow, waiting in line to check in, and I was as excited as I've ever been. I'd travelled a lot around the UK and Ireland but had never gone as far as the Caribbean. When we got to the front of the check-in line, the woman was going through the normal questions. She asked me if I'd packed my own bags and, for a reason I still can't quite fathom, I replied: 'Most of it.'

Yes. I know.

There was this moment where she looked up at me because nobody ever answers like that. Everyone mumbles a 'yes' and moves on. I tried to clarify that my husband had helped, but it was too late. By then, she was convinced we were international drug smugglers, so we were sent off to this side room where we had to unpack everything from our bags in front of this poor man from the airline. When I say everything, I mean EVERYTHING.

The entire time, your father was looking at me, not needing to say anything because I was thinking it anyway.

Of course, our bags were only full of the usual stuff and we repacked and managed to check in with time to spare.

That's not the story.

We were sitting on the plane, waiting for take-off. Everyone was strapped in, ready to go and life felt brilliant. The engines roared and there was this ripple of anticipation from everyone on board as we soared upwards. I think someone towards the back even clapped. The ground was shrinking and England turned into this wonderful expanse of green. It was utterly beautiful and I couldn't stop staring out the window.

Then, three rows ahead of us, this woman stood up. She'd got really short dark hair and she was pulling at it – then she started screaming. One of the flight attendants was trying to get her to sit because the seatbelt light was on, but she started shouting even louder. She was bellowing, 'Oh my God, we're all going to die!' at the top of her voice.

People tried to calm her, while others shouted at her to be quiet. She was ignoring everyone, pounding on the back of her seat, saying she fell asleep before take-off, and she'd had a dream in which the plane crashed and everyone died.

Eventually, the pilot came on and said he was turning the plane around because of 'an incident', which people actually laughed at – largely because the 'incident' was right in front of us.

We landed at Heathrow and the police came on board. They escorted the woman off but she was still shouting that everyone was going to die. I was watching everyone else, fascinated by the different reactions. Some people were really angry that this woman had cost them an hour or so of their lives. They were shouting abuse back and clapping as she was taken away. Others said nothing, staring at their feet or out the window. Most people were whispering quietly to each other. It was a really strange atmosphere.

Then something happened that I've never been able to explain. Out of nowhere, I felt really itchy. Not in one spot, but over my entire body. I knew so clearly that I could not be on the plane.

I told your father this and he gulped, then he said that, if I wanted to get off, he'd stay with me. I unclipped my seatbelt and approached one of the stewardesses, saying that I wanted to leave.

Then another woman did the same.

Then a man.

Then a couple.

In no time, half the people on the plane wanted off. Some were running, some crying, others just left with this blank nothingness on their face.

Of course, the plane did not crash and nobody died.

We've never had a holiday abroad and the reason we've given you – that I am scared of flying – is perfectly true. It's hard to describe. I know it's utterly irrational, that there's probably more chance of being hit by lightning or being pecked to death by a swan than there is of dying in a plane crash, but sometimes irrational fears rule the mind.

We did other things instead, as you'll remember. Most summers when you were little, your father and I took you to the coast for a week or so. We'd hire a caravan, or get a bed and breakfast. Occasionally, we went to Scotland or Wales. We took the train to France once. It wasn't the money that stopped us from going further, it was a lack of desire.

Which is why it feels so strange now. When I was younger and more capable, I was only interested in my small corner of the world. Now I can barely get out of bed, I suddenly have an urge to see everything.

Every parent wants the best for their child and I suppose all I can say is this: if you get the chance to visit new places and meet new people, say yes every time. Life without other people isn't life at all.

I hope this finds you well. Two little ducks and all that. Happy birthday,

Mum

PS: If you do get married and have a honeymoon, whatever you do, don't spend it painting the spare room. Been there, done that. It's not much fun.

Almost forty minutes passed before Mark returned to Poppy's side on the grass. He was yawning, carrying a supermarket bag over his wrist and cupping two pints with his hands. 'I have no idea why they take so many pictures,' he said, passing Poppy another cider.

'Because if they take five of a similar thing, they can pick the best one.'

Mark supped the top of his pint. 'Don't take their side!'

They laughed and then Mark lay flat on his back. There was a long pause in which Poppy stared off into the distance, looking at nothing and yet everything. It was so green, so beautiful. There was a stile at the edge of the beer garden, which led into a huge expanse of field. A pair of hikers could be seen bounding along in the distance, walking sticks stabbing into the ground every few paces.

Poppy could feel Mark watching her but she didn't trust herself to look at him, didn't know if she'd say something she shouldn't. She'd kept all her mother's letters and sometimes reread the one telling her not to burn bridges, to think before she spoke. It had felt important back when she'd first read it; it felt even more so now.

'We don't talk anywhere near enough,' Mark said.

'My phone number hasn't changed.'

He sighed. 'I know. I'm not saying it's your fault. It's completely mine. Things have been busy and now you've come all the way up here on your birthday. I can't say thank you enough.'

Poppy let his words settle for a moment. 'What else was I going to do?' she said, eventually.

Mark sat up and reached into his bag.

'Speaking of birthdays…'

He took out a familiar-shaped rectangle wrapped in frog-patterned yellow paper and passed it over.

'I wrapped it myself,' he said.

'I wonder what it could be,' Poppy replied, smiling. She didn't open it, instead putting it into a pocket of her bag. 'Thank you.'

'You are absolutely welcome.'

'I've almost used up last year's – and the ones from the year before.'

'You've been busy! How is art class?'

'Fun. Something different every fortnight. There are a lot of nice people there. One of the women got a grant from the council last month. They're paying for her to put on a display in one of their galleries. It's a really big deal.'

Mark nodded along. 'You'll be next.'

'You haven't seen how good she is.' There was a short pause as they each had a drink, and then Poppy added, 'You looking forward to tomorrow?'

'Of course!'

Poppy didn't need to reply. She raised an eyebrow and Mark continued, 'I'm bricking it. I'm looking forward to the whole actually-being-married-thing – but did you see how many people were on her side of the church at the rehearsal? There'll be even more tomorrow. Then I've got to give a speech in the evening.'

'You've had twenty-odd years of practising how to talk. Haven't you got it nailed by now?'

'Not in front of three hundred people. And not in front of Iris's mum.' Mark swigged his cider but there were worry lines creasing his forehead.

'She does seem a bit intense,' Poppy said.

'That's one word for it.' Mark peered over his shoulder and then pushed himself up slightly higher so that he could look around to make sure Iris's family weren't close enough to overhear. 'Iris is a bit *different* when her mum's around. Remember when I said her parents run a café? That's only part of it. They've got a coffee shop on the harbour but they also own another half-dozen in the area, and they run a catering business that serves the entire north-east. They employ about eighty people and own a second house in the south of France.'

'So?'

'So… I'm the outsider who's stealing away their only daughter. Her dad has just about accepted that I'm not a total monster, but her mum…'

'She can't be that bad?'

He sighed. 'I don't know… Maybe not – it might just be because of the whole wedding thing. She's trying to micro-manage everything and that gets Iris stressed, then it all starts to fall apart. It's why today was such a release. But then we're back here with four photographers, and her friends giving me dirty looks for talking to you instead of them…'

Poppy glanced over towards Iris's family and friends, none of whom were giving them anything remotely like a dirty look.

'You'll be fine after tomorrow,' Poppy said. 'It'll all go perfectly, everyone will love your speech and, when it's all done, you won't remember these nerves.'

Mark finished the rest of his drink and said he was going to the bar. Poppy watched him walking away, trying to remember if she had ever seen him like this before. He'd always been full of natural confidence because life was so easy for him. In one way, Poppy was relieved to discover that he was like her after all – fallible and capable of nerves – but it was also unsettling to see him riddled with self-doubt.

He returned a few minutes later with four more bottles of cider. He put three on the ground next to Poppy's chair and started swigging the other.

'At least it's going to be sunny tomorrow,' he said.

'Lots of outdoor pictures…'

Mark shook his head. 'Don't start…' He yawned, pinching the top of his nose and lowering his voice. 'How's Frey? I've not heard from her in ages. She de-friended me on Facebook and I figured that was that. I've still got her number but I didn't want to call or text.'

'She's working in a call centre, dealing with complaints for a mobile phone company.'

Mark winced. 'Ouch.'

'I'm not sure if I feel sorrier for her or the customers. She's moved in with a lad she met at work.'

There was the merest hesitation from Mark at this revelation; he didn't seem that surprised. 'But you're both still in Bristol?'

'Right. I see her a couple of times a week for a coffee or a cocktail. Once or twice she's fallen out with her fella and kipped on my sofa. You know Frey.'

Mark snorted. 'You sound relieved that you're not living together any more?'

Poppy swapped her empty cider bottle for a full one. 'It was a bit full-on at times. Seeing her a couple of times a week is brilliant. All day, every day? Not so much.'

Mark nodded, knowing this as well as anyone. 'And your database job?

'I didn't want to tell you online. I left six weeks ago. The structure wasn't quite what they made out and my manager was a bit of an arse. I wasn't enjoying it, so I left. I'd saved up a bit of money, so I'm OK.'

Poppy could feel Mark staring at her. She'd hoped he wouldn't notice, but he knew her too well. She continued gazing straight ahead, watching Iris's brother and father laughing at something, but she could feel Mark's eyes settle on her neck.

'What happened to your necklace?' he asked.

'I left it at home.'

He continued to stare and Poppy felt like he was extracting the truth from her memory, as if he somehow knew everything that had happened. She found it hard not to shiver, to wilt under the pressure.

'You didn't leave it at home, did you?' he asked quietly, still staring.

Poppy drank deeply from the bottle, enjoying the tangy bitterness. 'I was a bit short on rent.'

Mark sighed but said nothing more.

On the other side of the garden, Iris's brother was calling Mark's name, asking if he wanted something to drink. Mark held up his own bottle and shook his head. There was a momentary locking of eyes between them, Liam's gaze lingering a second too long as he seemed to query why Mark was spending so much time with a girl none of the others had previously met.

A girl he wasn't marrying the next day.

Liam eventually turned and headed into the pub, but it felt like a beckoning, as if Mark was expected to follow.

'Poppy…' Mark said her name so softly that there was suddenly a lump in Poppy's throat. Only he could say it like that.

'It'll work out,' Poppy replied, gulping back the lump. 'It's not like I was doing badly at the job. They offered me a promotion. A bit more money, some extra responsibility…'

'So why did you leave?'

'I wasn't happy. I wanted something different but wasn't sure what. If I'd taken the promotion, that would have been that. I'd have been forever working with databases, stuck behind a desk. A job that was supposed to have been temporary would, all of a sudden, have become my career. I figured that, if I left, it would force me to find something else.'

Mark didn't reply for a while. Poppy wondered if he disapproved. She had lied to Derek, to Freya, to everyone about what had happened. She hadn't wanted to receive the head-tilt and the advice everyone gave about not leaving steady work. The problem was that such advice wouldn't work for her. A craving for stability had left her stuck in a relationship with Clyde. It could also have seen her stranded in the town where she grew up. She needed to be forced into changes.

Mark nodded, accepting what she'd said. 'What about your dad?'

'I've not told him yet.' She turned to face him, still sensing his gaze burning her neck. 'Stop looking at me like that.'

He didn't shift. 'Like what?'

'Like I need rescuing. I'll figure it out. I'm not a snob – if I have to work as a cleaner or whatever, I'll do it. I couldn't stay in that office, though. I'd have gone crazy.'

It took another couple of seconds but Mark finally turned away. 'How *is* your dad?'

Poppy leaned back in the deckchair, stretching out her legs and started to laugh. 'He's getting remarried.'

'Really?'

'Later in the year – a winter wedding.'

She didn't look down but felt Mark's hand on her bare knee. It was clammy but reassuring. 'Are you OK with that?' he asked.

'Course I am. It'll be a bit strange but he's happy. Madeleine is nice, too. She keeps him in check. I'm worried they're going to ask me to do something. One minute you're happily minding your own business, the next they want you to do a reading or something.' She sat back up and patted Mark on the head. 'And you know what people say – public speaking is the absolute *worst* thing you can do. Imagine all the things that can go wrong…'

She grinned and he just about matched it. 'Thanks for your support.'

Poppy rolled to the side and unzipped the side pocket of her bag. She pulled out a small rectangular packet, wrapped in golden paper with a matching ribbon.

'I wrapped your wedding present,' she said, handing it over.

'I wrapped your *birthday* present.'

'I still don't believe you. You either got Iris to do it, or bribed someone in the shop. There's no way you're that neat.'

Mark reeled back with indignation. 'Get me a box and some paper right now and I'll prove it.'

They stared at each other and then burst out laughing at the same time.

'Open it now,' Poppy said.

Mark was twisting the gift in his hands. 'I should probably wait for Iris.'

'Tomorrow will be chaos.'

He didn't need telling twice, looping his fingers under the ribbon and pulling until it came loose. That done, he tore the paper apart. When the gift was uncovered he turned it around in his hands until it was the right way up, and then stared at it.

'Pops… This is beautiful.'

He turned around for her to see, even though she was the person who had drawn it. Using the pencils he'd given her, Poppy had sketched an image of Mark and Iris as she remembered them from the Blackpool seafront. There was a blob of ice cream on Mark's nose and Iris's face was creased with giggles.

'Iris is going to flip when she sees this,' Mark added.

'I didn't have much money, so that was all I could manage.'

He goggled at her. 'Are you serious? This is so much better than something you could have bought.'

Poppy shrugged. 'Are you sure you like it?'

'I mean it, Pops. Some of Iris's family will have spent hundreds on us. Thousands. You should see the bill for the wedding breakfast tomorrow – it's insane. Nothing's going to beat this, though.'

'If you say so.'

Mark rolled up onto his knees. He leaned forward and hugged Poppy, pressing his fingers into her back. Over his shoulder, she could see Iris's brother and father watching them, confusion simmering on each of their faces. She patted his back gently until he got the message and pulled away. For a moment he looked surprised, then Poppy nodded towards the other side of the garden and his expression cleared as he understood.

'I should probably mingle,' Mark whispered.

'I know.'

He stood, rocking from one foot to the other: Poppy on one side, his new family on the other.

'I'm really sorry,' he said.

'It's fine – go and socialise.'

He shook his head. 'Not for that.'

'For what?'

'I should've told you earlier…' He turned again, peering between Poppy and Iris's family. He grimaced, as if in pain.

Poppy felt a shiver ripple along her back. 'What?'

'There's another reason why Iris's mum is annoyed with us… I've been offered a job with a design company.'

'But that's good, right?'

'It's in Toronto. They've been working on the visa for a while. They're renting an apartment for us. We're moving to Canada in a few weeks. It was too good an offer to turn down.'

Poppy stared up at him from the chair, a lump forming again in her throat. She could barely believe this was how he'd chosen to tell her.

'How long have you known?' she whispered.

'A couple of months. I wanted to tell you in person.' He took a half-step away. 'The world's so small now, though – mobiles, texts, Skype and all that. We'll be able to talk all the time.'

Poppy breathed in through her nose, holding her breath, not moving. 'You should go,' she said. 'You've got a big day tomorrow.'

Twenty-Three

Poppy pulled the hoody up and off over her head and then tied it around her waist. 'I thought Canada was cold all the time?' she said, smoothing her hair down.

Mark laughed – but then he was wearing shorts and a T-shirt. 'Who told you that?'

'I don't know – you hear Canada, you think snow. I thought Toronto would be cold. I brought all my winter stuff.'

He glanced sideways, half-smiling in the way he always did at her. That knowing, too-smart-for-his-own-good-look he'd had since he was six years old. 'Why didn't you check the weather report?' he said. 'Or ask?'

Poppy shrugged. 'Because sensible people do that. *Boring* people.'

'True.'

Mark waited on the edge of the pavement, tugging on Poppy's sleeve as she went to step into the road. 'Whoa,' he said.

Poppy stepped backwards, peering both ways along the empty road. 'There's nothing coming.'

He nodded at the red stop light on the other side of the street. 'They have that weird jay-walking law here. You have to wait for the walk signal.'

'Even when there's nothing coming?'

'Yep. When we first moved here, the agency had one of the locals show me around. He reckons he once got fined for crossing on red.'

'They made him *pay* for crossing the road?'

'That's what he said.'

'Is Canada run by Nazis?' Poppy pulled free of his grasp and started to cross. Mark hurried after her, running to keep up and then slowing as they reached the opposite pavement.

'Ooooh, walking on the wild side,' Poppy teased. 'Best lock me up with all the murderers.'

Mark rolled his eyes. 'It's good to see you,' he said.

'Yes,' she agreed. 'It's good to see you too.'

They continued across a lush bank of grass until they reached a paved area, where Poppy stopped to stare up at a statue. It was of a large set of scales that looked like a giant seesaw. On one side was a lion, on the other was a lamb. Despite the lion being far larger, the scales were perfectly balanced.

Poppy stepped closer and read out loud: '"Every individual is equal before and under the law and has the right to the equal protection and equal benefit of the law without discrimination."' She nodded and turned to Mark. 'It's a bit more poetic than someone graffitiing "your mum" at the bottom of the stairs where I live.'

He smiled and pointed up at the building beyond. 'This is the courthouse,' he said.

Poppy turned to study it. 'I like it. I'd probably like it even more if I wasn't wearing jeans in thirty-degree heat.'

'Come on,' Mark said, 'this way.'

Poppy looked up at him as they walked. His hair was shorter and neater, and he had a hint of a belly coming along – but otherwise, Mark hadn't changed much in the year since Poppy had last seen him.

When he'd first moved, he had been so busy with the new country and new job that she'd wondered if they would ever be back in regular contact. Then, three or four months previously, things had changed. It had suddenly been as if they were the best of friends again. He'd send Poppy a message and when she got back to him he'd reply instantly. She'd wake up most mornings to a message he'd sent late at night.

They Skyped a couple of times a week, talking about nothing and everything – but it was the nothing that really counted. Mark hardly ever mentioned Iris. He talked about his job and his workmates, or wanted to know what was popular on UK television so that he could hunt it down. He talked about going to ice hockey matches, baseball games, or the movies he'd seen that were yet to cross the Atlantic.

Then he'd asked if she fancied visiting and, spurred on by her mother's words – *if you get the chance to visit new places and meet new people, say yes every time* – Poppy had agreed.

Poppy tugged at the long sleeves of her sweatshirt now, wishing she *had* looked at the weather report before leaving England. If the heat continued, she'd have to buy new clothes, else she'd sweat away half her body weight.

'This is a different kind of heat to what I've experienced before,' she said as she walked next to Mark.

'What are you on about?'

'I've been to Ibiza. It's hot there, but not like this.'

'If it's hot, it's hot.'

'I don't know how to explain it.'

Mark nudged her with his elbow. 'I'm messing with you. This is city heat. It's not only warm, you've got the heat of the cars, the people, the air-conditioner emissions, plus the humidity coming from Lake Ontario.' He waved a hand in front of them. 'Either that or the city's built on an underground volcano.' He paused to readjust his sunglasses. 'This is the furthest away from home you've been, isn't it?'

'I suppose,' Poppy replied quietly. 'I'd not thought about it.'

They reached another crosswalk, but this time there was a small crowd of people waiting. Poppy got into line behind them, mouthing the word 'Nazis' at Mark.

'What?' he asked.

'Nazis,' she whispered.

'Huh?'

'Nazis,' Poppy repeated, much louder.

Mark grinned as the three women in front of them turned to look at Poppy. They sported the same frown and then turned to face the road again.

Mark leaned in. 'Gotcha.'

Poppy stifled a smile and turned towards the road, where a succession of bicycles and cars were zipping past. A steady stream of car horns sounded from a street or two away and then, as if to answer the mating call, the cars in front of them began honking. Poppy had thought the image of square blocks and hooting horns was an American cliché – but here it was in front of her, alive and well in Canada.

The traffic eventually parted and they crossed. They stop-started their way across a few more blocks until they rounded a building, heading onto the edge of a plaza where Poppy stopped and stared upwards.

'Big, isn't it?' Mark said as he joined her and looked up.

'If nothing else,' Poppy replied, 'we can definitely agree on the fact that it's big.'

'The CN Tower is one of the seven modern wonders of the world.'

Poppy continued staring. The tower was an enormous spike jabbed into the ground. It soared up and up. There was an observation bowl around two-thirds of the way up, and then it kept climbing some more. Mark and Poppy were standing in the sunlight but the shadow of the tower stretched close by, seeping into the distance for as far as Poppy could see.

'What are the other six?' Poppy asked.

Mark bit his lip. 'As soon as I told you that fact, I knew you'd ask for the other six.'

'You don't know them?'

'I think the Empire State Building might be one, maybe the Channel Tunnel. I don't know the others.'

'You'd be useless in a pub quiz. What other poorly researched facts do you half-know?'

Mark laughed. 'I know it was the tallest tower on Earth until 2010.'

'What happened in 2010?'

'Someone built a bigger one.'

She poked him under the ribs, making him squirm. 'I always forget how annoying you are. Anything else?'

'It's five hundred and something metres high.'

'*Something?* Do you think that's how they measured it out? "All right, lads. Let's aim for five hundred and something metres and see how we do"?'

'Big though, isn't it?'

Poppy stared up again, shielding her eyes from the haze of the sun. 'It's definitely big.'

She turned, peering back the way they'd come and then twisting in a full circle. Banked steps led down to a larger paved area where there was an aquarium and, on the other side of the road, a stretch of grass. Cars were backed up in both directions and there were people as far as Poppy could see. All around, there were couples and groups posing for photographs and selfies, framed by the steeple behind.

'There're probably more people on this bit of concrete than there are in the whole of Purley,' Poppy said.

Mark placed a hand on her arm. 'Are you all right?'

'It's just so… big,' Poppy said. 'There are so many people.'

'Don't you like it?'

'I don't know… Maybe. I can't take it all in.' Poppy continued looking around, but it felt as though the noise was rising. Cars, people, the hum of a city. Bristol was busy; Blackpool in that singular moment of summer sun was crazy… but this was another step up again. It was all so big and she felt like the merest of insignificant specks, lost among the horde.

She took Mark's hand. 'Take me somewhere real,' Poppy said. 'Away from the billboards, the tourists and the beep-beep-beep of the car horns.'

His fingers interlocked with hers. He squeezed her hand gently before he released it. 'Everywhere's a bit beep-beep-beepy.'

'You must know somewhere? You've been here for ten months.'

'Do you mind walking?'

'Nope.'

He nodded past the tower. 'Let's go, then.'

Mark and Poppy weaved through the crowds, sometimes stopping at the crosswalks, sometimes walking anyway – Nazis be damned. They headed across a wide four-lane road and then turned onto a small street, where the crowds were thinner. The hum of the city started to dim as the heights of the buildings dropped. The roads narrowed, the shops shrank, and it felt like they had crossed into a smaller town.

'Where are we?' Poppy asked.

'This is still Toronto. There are lots of different areas.' Mark nodded ahead. 'When we cross that road, we'll be in Kensington Market.'

'I don't know what that is.'

'You'll see.'

Poppy smelled it before she saw it. As they turned past a small row of parked cars, something spicy yet fruity caught on the breeze. Poppy sniffed the air. 'What's that?'

'Something good.'

The street was full of cars parked nose to tail on one side of the road. On the other, people were weaving bicycles effortlessly in and out of pedestrians, who weren't even attempting to walk on the pavement. Small two-storey buildings lined both sides of the street. It felt very familiar, very English.

The smell got stronger until they rounded another corner and then Poppy saw where it was coming from. Outside a glass-fronted store, a man was cooking on an upturned oil drum that had been converted into a grill. Steam billowed into the air as a flame licked high. The man was wearing a red, white and green woollen beanie with sunglasses. He laughed as he batted at the flame, before he flipped a blackened leg of chicken onto a waiting customer's plate.

'Rasta Pasta,' Poppy said, reading the sign over the shop.

'Someone from my agency put me onto this place,' Mark said. 'They do amazing jerk chicken and fish with spicy pasta. The first time I came here, I was so full, I didn't think I'd be able to stand up. I actually think it might be criminal if you fly all this way and don't try it.'

Poppy wasn't about to argue, but she added, 'Not quite traditional Canadian cuisine, is it?'

'We can get you some poutine before you leave.'

'What's that?'

Mark's face lit up. 'Layer of chips, layer of gravy, layer of cheese curd, layer of gravy. Then repeat over and over. Add some meat on top and it's the greatest food known to man.'

Poppy's stomach gurgled. 'I can see why you moved to Canada.'

After they'd eaten, Mark led Poppy through the rest of the area around Kensington Market. It felt like a village within the city. The streets became ever narrower. Cars slowly edged among the pedestrians, who made little effort to stay off the roads.

So much for being fined for crossing the street, Poppy thought.

The bakeries reeked of fresh bread, there were two separate shops selling nothing but cheese, and then there was an old woman standing on the street selling fruit and nuts from enormous barrels. The smells and sounds made it feel like a daytime street party, but it was only a couple of blocks until they were walking among houses again, like any other town.

'I saw your online shop,' Mark said as they walked.

'It makes a bit of money here and there,' Poppy replied. 'I sell through eBay, Etsy and a couple of other places, plus redirect people to my own site.'

'I thought tech wasn't your thing?'

'It's not, but it was easier than I thought. Frey's been really helpful.'

For a moment, Poppy thought that Mark was going to query whether it was possible for Freya to be helpful – but he didn't. He'd not seen Freya in almost five years, she realised. She was ancient history to him now.

'How does it feel selling your artwork?'

'What d'you mean?'

'I don't know… Doesn't it feel a little strange to create something and then send it off to a stranger, never to be seen again?'

Poppy stopped walking, standing still on the pavement. They had reached a larger main road and were outside a doughnut shop. 'I've never thought of it like that,' she said.

'How do you think of it?'

'I was more concerned with paying rent and buying food.'

Mark puffed out his bottom lip and nodded. 'Can't argue with that.'

'I don't only sell originals. You can get prints put on anything nowadays. If people like something I've done, they can order it on mugs, T-shirts, socks, underwear, all sorts.'

'*Underwear*? Someone's walking around with one of your drawings on their bum?'

'Or their crotch.'

Mark laughed. 'When I get home, I'm ordering a pair of your boxers. I'm going to wait until it's really warm – the hottest day of the year – and then I'm going to layer up to get them nice and sweaty.'

She slapped him with the back of her hand. 'You're disgusting.'

'How much do you make from this sordid underwear business?'

She whacked him again. 'Oi! It's not an underwear business and it's not sordid. Anyway, don't you know it's rude to ask about money?'

'We've already established that I'm a disgusting individual.'

'True. All right, I do OK. I'm not rolling in it, not living the high life in a big city like *some* people, but I get by. I make enough to buy food, pay rent and afford an air ticket here. I'm making more than I used to at the office, plus I can get up when I want. I had two original commissions in the past three months – and each of them made what would've been a week's salary in my old job.'

Mark let out a long, low whistle. 'What's that? Twenty minutes' work? Half-hour? Quick, easy sketch and away you go?'

Poppy slapped him one final time. 'Hey! You're supposed to be my supportive friend. My rock. My shoulder to cry on. It's more work than my old job.'

Mark grinned and put his arm around her, then instantly pulled away. 'Ick, sweaty,' he said. 'You know I'm only joking.'

'Luckily for you, I do. I'm always up to something, though. If I'm not working on a piece, then I'm off to the post office, or buying packing supplies. Then I've got all the emails and payments to handle. Plus I have to work out my own tax. How mad is that? I hardly understand any of it.'

'You're enjoying it, though?'

She took his arm and they continued along the street. 'I've had worse jobs.'

Poppy's feet were beginning to ache as they continued along the road. It stretched as far as she could see: one long straight line in a grid of long, straight lines. The shops, cafés and restaurants had given way to tree-lined roads, with parked cars on both sides and rows of two- and three-storey detached houses. Shadows drenched both sides of the street and, for the first time that day, Poppy was feeling comfortable in her long trousers.

'Where are we going?' she asked.

'Home.'

'How far away is it?'

'Is that an adult way of asking, "Are we there yet?"'

'Maybe.'

'Five minutes.'

Poppy was counting down the seconds as they crossed the road and headed away on a road perpendicular to where they had been going. It wasn't long before Mark stopped to lean against a lamp-post. He nodded at the house in front of them.

'What do you reckon?' he asked.

The house had two main storeys with a triangular window in the attic. It looked like it had been renovated recently, the shiny white paint yet to be dirtied by a winter of bad weather. At the front was a small garden and there was a path that led along the side, offering a glimpse of a far larger yard at the back.

'It's big,' Poppy said.

'Not CN Tower-big, but definitely big. There's a basement, too – so we've got four floors. The company is paying the rent and it's fully furnished. Almost none of it is ours, but it's a great place. We'd have had you staying with us but the agency offers to put up a guest on our behalf four times a year, so I figured you might as well enjoy a swanky hotel.' He pointed over the top of the house. 'We've gone the long way round but it's only a twenty-five minute walk to where I work. Five or ten minutes past that to the main downtown area.'

She gave him a crooked look. '"Downtown"? Have you gone native?'

'Fine! To the city centre. Happy?'

'Delirious.'

Mark was about to say something else when his phone started to ring. He plucked it from his pocket and frowned at whatever he saw on the screen. He turned his back as he answered and sputtered a series of 'yes' or 'no' replies.

When he turned back to Poppy, his expression had darkened. 'Sorry. I was going to give you the house tour but Iris needs me. She's at the zoo but doesn't like driving in the city, and her bus…' He tailed off. 'Sorry.'

Poppy shrugged. 'Things happen.'

Mark was speaking too quickly. 'She's not really settling, and she's missing her mum and dad. She's not been able to get a proper job because there's this whole thing going on with her visa. Then I'm not home a lot and today's one of the few days I'm not at the office – but you're here, so…' He subsided again. 'I didn't mean it like that.'

'I know.'

'She's just lonely.'

'It's fine.'

He rubbed his forehead with the back of his hand. His eyes looked tired. 'I'll drive you back to your hotel, then pick her up. We're still on for dinner, though?'

'Of course.'

'And you know where we're meeting?'

Poppy held up her own phone. 'I know the name and I've got some apps. I'll figure it out. I'll see you at eight.'

'I'll still give you a lift.'

Poppy shook her head, even though her feet were aching. 'You go. I don't want to get you in any more trouble.'

His features sank. 'Don't be like that.'

'I'm not being like anything. It's fine – you go. I want to explore. I'll see you both at eight.'

'Are you sure?'

'I'm going to stop at the one of the cafés on the way back. There's something I have to do.'

Mark had one hand on the side of the black 4x4 that was parked outside the house.

'Go,' Poppy said.

So he did.

My dearest Poppy,

I don't know if you're still reading these letters but, if you are, I suppose you're wondering when I'm going to finally get to the bit where you come along. Rest assured, I'm nearly there.

Nearly.

I'll skip past the gory details you won't want to hear but your father and I had been hoping I'd get pregnant for a while. We'd been trying with no luck, so we visited a specialist doctor. Tests went on and on and they could not figure out what was wrong with either of us. In the end, it was nothing but stress.

Meanwhile – largely because of that – things were not great at home between your father and I. The house was 'finished' in the sense that we'd been repairing and renovating for years and we had finally got to a point where there wasn't much left to do. Your father was bored with his job and I'd been doing mine for a while. We felt like we were ready for something else, wanting more from our lives than what we had. Children were the next step but that wasn't happening, which left us in a strange place. There was nothing particularly wrong, but it felt like we were going through the motions.

So we stopped talking to one another.

It happened over time. For instance, instead of talking about our days after work, we'd put the TV on and watch that. We used to visit the cinema once a week but got out of the habit and didn't restart. Sometimes I'd cook, sometimes your father would. We might watch TV, or read – but it was like we were living two separate lives under one roof. We never fell out, never really argued; we simply drifted apart.

It all culminated on a Wednesday that I'll never forget. Your father was working away from home, staying for a night in a hotel on the south coast, in Paignton. I was sitting at home by myself, reading a book but taking nothing in. I'd read a page, then realise I'd not actually read a word. I'd try again but still not take any of it on board. I remember thinking, 'What am I doing? What are we doing?' – and I didn't have an answer.

So I got in the car and drove.

This was before mobile phones and apps, so I was using a map and relying on road signs. I was aiming for Paignton but ended up in Plymouth, which is thirty miles away. I only realised this when it was already dark and I went past the 'Welcome to Plymouth' sign. I turned around, but it was all small country lanes and, for reasons you now understand, that made me nervous.

It took me far longer than it should have done but I eventually reached the place your father was staying. It was a chain hotel on the edge of the town but there was no twenty-four-hour front desk, and it was after eleven by the time I arrived. All the lights were off, the doors were locked and I had no idea what to do.

He had called to let me know he was there safely but I'd not heard the telephone. Yes, that's an ancient telephone with a wire connected to the wall. He'd left a message on the answer machine to say he was staying in room 113, but that was all I knew. From that, I assumed he was on the first floor. There was a row of windows at the front of the building, another at the back. I thought that if room 101 was the first window closest to reception on the front of the building, then 102 would be the first window on the back.

It was a bit of a guess, but if I was right, then your father was staying in the seventh window along.

If I was right…

I started to flick these tiny stones at the seventh window along – except that I was terrible and kept missing. I'd got stones pinging off the wall, the gutters, the roof. I'm not exaggerating – more stones bounced down and hit me than ever hit the glass.

A face finally appeared at the window – except that it wasn't your father's. It belonged to this poor old bloke in a dressing gown. He opened the window as best he could but it wouldn't go all the way, so he shouted down, asking what I wanted. I said I'd locked myself out of my room and could he be really kind and let me in?

And he did!

He came down still wearing the dressing gown, which showed off his hairy, veiny knees. He was really kind and I felt terrible for lying to him. He let me in and said I must be freezing, that sort of thing. He went back up in the lift, so I took the stairs. I waited a bit out of sight until he'd gone back into his room and then I went to room 113 – which turned out to be directly opposite this old man's. I didn't want him to come into the corridor again, so I knocked on your father's door really softly.

Nothing happened.

I tried again, just gentle tip-taps, trying to be as quiet as I could, but he still wasn't answering the door. I stood there for about five minutes, trying various combinations of calm door-knocks, hoping to find a way he'd hear me. I was getting to the point where I thought I'd have to knock loudly and make something up if anyone else came out of their rooms – and then room 113 opened.

It wasn't your father – it was this woman I'd never seen before. Her hair was a mess and she was yawning. I should probably be ashamed of this but my first thought was, 'Oh my God, Chris is seeing someone else' – but then I saw a different bloke behind her, peering out into the corridor.

Turned out, I was in the wrong hotel. It was part of a chain, with hotels on both sides of the town, and I'd mixed them up.

I was mortified and apologised about a dozen times, before running out of the hotel. I now had the address for the other one and, when I got there, it did have a twenty-four-hour front desk. I breezed in as if I was a guest, went upstairs, and knocked on room 113. Your father opened the door almost immediately. He was still up and it was like he'd been waiting for me. We didn't have to say anything at that point because we both knew we'd been stupid.

From then on, we've been a lot better about making time for one another – even if that was only going to the cinema together, or finding time for a meal out.

Over time, friends will come and go. There's nothing particularly wrong with that; it's how life is. But there will also be a handful of people with whom you share a special connection. You might not agree on everything, you might even tire of one another – but when times are hard, those are the people that will always be there for you. Treasure that, Pops.

As well as that, I learned one more thing. If you're going to visit a hotel in the middle of the night, you should double-check the address.

Happy birthday.

Mum

Poppy enjoyed being by herself in the unfamiliar city. She walked along Queen Street, popping into the various independent clothes shops, where she found herself a skirt that was much more comfortable than the jeans. She treated herself to a velvety chocolate croissant in a bakery opposite the CTV studios and then continued walking.

It wasn't long before she found herself in the shadow of the CN Tower once more. Figuring she might never get the chance again, Poppy crossed the plaza and got in line to buy a ticket that would take her up to the viewing platform. She fiddled with her phone as she edged forward at regular intervals, while snatching snippets of the conversations around her. One woman was arguing with her daughter over where they were going to eat later in the day, while a large man was complaining about the state of Canadian beer – which was a bit of a cheek, Poppy thought, considering he had an American drawl.

Poppy was soon in a lift being whooshed up the tower, the buildings below shrinking to doll's houses as she watched through the glass window. It felt like seconds before the doors were opening behind her, with the guide pointing Poppy towards a second elevator. After another queue and a minute or so in the other lift, she stepped out onto the SkyPod level.

There was glass everywhere Poppy looked, angled towards the ground and offering a view so incredible that she didn't know where to focus her attention. Couples and families crept around the circular viewing deck, pressing against the front and posing for photographs. Poppy found a spot close to an Asian couple and stared out at the blue expanse of Lake Ontario bleeding into the horizon. There was a small triangular island directly ahead and minuscule pinprick boats zipping across the water.

Poppy sidestepped around the platform until she found herself gazing across an ocean of concrete and glass. The city was laid out like a three-dimensional crossword puzzle, with long straight lines split into squares stretching far into the distance. Humans had become ants, scuttling about their business, unaware they were being spied upon from above.

As she continued around the circle, Poppy was unsure where to look because everything was so incredible. She eventually found herself close to where she'd started, staring across the wonder of the lake. She was focusing on a boat in the distance when it suddenly felt as if the ground was hurtling towards her. Poppy felt her head spinning and clamped her eyes closed, taking a small step backwards to steady herself.

'Careful…'

Poppy felt a hand on her lower back and blinked her eyes open. The hand removed itself but she could sense it close by, ready to support her.

'You all right?' the male voice added.

'I went dizzy,' Poppy said.

The stars were clearing around the edges of her vision, allowing her to properly see the man in front of her. He was a little taller than her – a couple of years older, too – with straw-like shaggy hair and dark wispy hairs on his chin. He looked like he had recently fallen out of bed.

'We *are* a long way up,' he said.

Now that she'd regained her senses, Poppy caught the incline at the end of his sentence, as if he was asking her a question.

'Are you an Aussie?' she asked, changing the subject.

'What gave me away?'

'The flip-flops.'

The man glanced at his feet and then shrugged. 'Fair point. I'm Bruce and I love shrimps on the barbie. What's your name?'

'There's no way you're named Bruce.'

He winked. 'Nah, it's Neil – but I had you going for a bit, didn't I?'

Poppy shook her head.

'You want your picture taking?' he asked.

'Huh?'

He nodded around them. '*Everyone's* having their picture taken. Within the hour, their friends will be getting bored stupid by an endless stream of Facebook photos.'

Poppy turned to see that he was right. Kids and adults alike were not simply enjoying the view, but absorbing a watered-down version through a tiny screen. No point in enjoyment if the illusion of a happy life couldn't be shared with everyone else, Poppy thought.

Neil mimed the clicking of a camera shutter with his hands. 'So do you want me to do the deed?'

'I think my friends will live if they don't see me grinning like a lunatic.'

'Suit yourself – my friends will definitely *not* live without pictures of this face in various places they've never been.' He offered her his phone with a grin. 'It does have that front-camera selfie mode thing but I always end up taking pictures angled up my nose and nobody needs to see that. I have got a good nose, though.'

Poppy wasn't sure what having a good nose entailed but she supposed if it involved not being crooked, overly large, or flattened, then Neil was doing OK. She took his phone and scooted around as he posed in front of the lake, giving the obligatory double-V for peace signs.

When she was done, she handed the phone back and he checked the image. 'I'm not a weirdo, by the way,' he said.

'In my experience, that's what weirdoes say.'

Neil indicated straight ahead. 'In that case, I'm going to change the subject by pointing out that you can see Niagara Falls in the distance. You have to squint a bit but it is there.'

Poppy stepped closer to the glass, narrowing her eyes and trying to focus on the blue and white dot touching the horizon in the direction he'd indicated. '*That's* Niagara Falls?' she asked.

'Have you ever been?'

'No.'

'It's very wet.'

Poppy continued gazing into the distance, wondering if the small streaks of movement genuinely were the gushing of the waterfall. It was vaguely in the right direction and it would have been an odd thing to make up, so he was probably right.

Neil was still staring out towards Lake Ontario. 'Why are you here by yourself?' he asked.

'My friend had to go and do something. Why are *you* on your own?'

Poppy felt him shrug beside her. 'I travel alone.'

'Ah,' she replied. 'You're one of *them*.'

'One of who?'

'Gap-year types. Always travelling. You're into yoga and meditating, aren't you? You eat quinoa and kale salads.'

He turned to her but Poppy continued staring through the glass. She knew he was grinning.

'Actually, Little Miss Judgey, I work as an adventure travel agent at home so often end up visiting new places by myself. I've been in the Canadian Rockies for two weeks and I'm going the long way home.'

Poppy smiled, knowing she'd heard the teensiest amount of defensiveness in his tone.

'What do you do?' he asked.

'I draw.'

'Draw what?'

'Things. People. Whatever interests me.'

'Could you sketch me?'

She turned to face him. His hair was messier than before and she suspected he'd ruffled his hand through it on purpose. 'People *always* ask that,' she said. 'If you tell them you draw, they want you to draw them. Tell them you write and they want a character based on them. Tell them you're a journalist and they've got a story for you.'

'You didn't answer the question.'

'I'm not in the mood and I don't have time.'

Neil tilted his head, puffing his bottom lip out. 'You said you draw things that interest you, so does this mean you don't find me interesting?' He screwed his features into a put-on look of hurt that made it seem like he might cry. It was so pathetic that Poppy couldn't hold back the laugh. As she broke, he cracked into a grin, too. He took his phone out of his pocket with one hand and put the other arm around her shoulders. If it was somebody else, Poppy thought, this might have been creepy, but Neil had an effortless charm.

'Let's have a pic then,' he said, stretching his phone out in front of them. Poppy could see them both on the screen.

'I thought you said you always end up taking selfies that angle up your nose?'

'Yeah – but I also said I have a good nose.'

Neil clicked the picture and then stepped away. 'So, tell me…' he said. 'You're on top of one of the world's greatest cities. This structure is one of the pinnacles of human achievement. Some people will go their entire lives not seeing anything like this. This tower is literally one of the wonders of the world – yet I have to bring my absolute A-game to even make you crack a smile?'

'Perhaps you're not as funny as you think?'

He stared at her, but his expression had changed subtly: lips no longer creased into a full smile, brown eyes sparkling with interest. He nodded past her, speaking a little more softly. 'You can walk that way back to the lift and I can go the other way. After this, we can never see or talk to one another again. Why not tell a total stranger your problems? What have you got to lose?'

Poppy continued meeting his gaze, then she reached out and took his hand, leading him around the circle until they were facing the centre of the city. 'Downtown', as Mark would call it. Poppy released Neil's hand and then stood shoulder to shoulder alongside him, peering across the vast expanse of human achievement. More couples and families were shuffling around them, taking photos, pointing and marvelling at the wonder of what was below.

'You first,' she said.

She felt him take a breath and, when he replied, his tone was harder than before. His accent was stronger when he wasn't trying to be cocky. 'I suppose I'm afraid of being alone,' he said. 'In the end, I mean. At the moment, I like being by myself. I like travelling and being able to go where I want – but I don't think I want it to be like this forever. I want that other person to share everything with.'

'There must be some Aussie girls who like the whole hair-like-a-bird's-nest thing?'

He shrugged but didn't laugh. 'Maybe, Little Miss Judgey, but perhaps I don't like them?' He took another breath. 'Your turn.'

Poppy focused on what would be a massive glass tower if she was on the ground. From where she was, it was merely a speck a bit larger than everything surrounding it. To its side, an orange crane was swinging sideways. Now that she was looking properly, there were cranes everywhere. It felt like the entire city was still being built.

'Life's passing me by,' she said quietly. 'Everything seems to be happening to *other* people. I grew up in this little village with two people who've been my best friends my whole life. Mark's gone from that to living here with his wife and an amazing job. My other friend, Freya, always has something going on. It's like she lives in a soap opera. She goes from boy to boy, from job to job. Somehow she always lands on her feet. She's pregnant now. I've got one best friend living halfway around the world, another who's going to be a mum. Even my dad's remarrying. In among all that, I'm existing. I'm in the middle, treading water. Going nowhere, doing nothing. No boyfriend, no kids, no proper career, no plans…'

She gulped, unsure what to add.

Neil said nothing for a while, taking in her story. 'Do you want any of those things?' he asked eventually.

'I don't know.'

'There's no shame in being the glue.'

She turned to him. 'Being the what?'

Neil faced her, eyes deep with sincerity. 'You're the glue,' he said. 'All these people around you have lives filled with drama. Every day, it's drama, drama, drama. You've got other friends, right?'

Poppy thought of Derek and the others from the gallery. 'I suppose.'

'You've had boyfriends, flings, wild nights of red-hot passion?'

'I'm not sure that's any of your business…'

He winked. 'So what's wrong with being the person in the middle? The one who has a normal, *enjoyable* life? Everyone else stumbles from disaster to disaster; shambles to shambles. You're the one who holds it all together. If you have friends around you – people you like, people who like you – what's wrong with that?'

Poppy tried to think. It felt like he'd simplified it too much. 'I don't know.'

'There's nothing wrong with being the glue, Poppy Pop.' Neil turned back to the window and took a deep breath. 'I'd *love* to be the glue.'

It took Poppy at least twenty seconds to realise that the entire menu was in Italian. She had scanned it once, picking out crossover words like 'spaghetti' and 'penne', but the fact none of it was in English had somehow escaped her. The one thing she *definitely* understood was the prices. Even allowing for the conversion back into British pounds, this was one very expensive place to eat.

Poppy returned to the start of the menu, trying to figure out at least one thing she might want to eat. Did 'pesce' mean fish? If so, there was some sort of fishy spaghetti dish, and a pizza, too. That wasn't a bad start.

She peered up at the sound of voices. The immaculately dressed waiter was leading Mark and Iris to the table, but they were muttering under their breaths to each other. Poppy barely caught the end of Iris's sentence – '… at the office' – before the two of them went silent. Mark was in smart trousers and a plain white shirt; Iris was wearing a long black dress that stretched to her ankles, with platform sandals. It was the first time Poppy had seen Iris since the wedding and she was surprised at how tired she looked. Mark's wife had made little effort to conceal the dark rings under her eyes, and there were the beginnings of lighter, greyer hairs poking through her fringe. The hippy-gypsy-summer style had disappeared, too. The fun and joy with which she'd glowed when they'd first met in Blackpool was gone.

From frowns, Mark and Iris both quickly changed to smiles and open-armed greetings as if a switch had been flicked. Poppy stood up to hug them and then they all sat.

'Are you enjoying the city?' Iris asked.

'Very much so,' Poppy replied. 'It's big but there are places where you don't feel it.'

'How's the hotel?'

'Brilliant. It has a separate living room. It's nicer than my flat at home. Thank you for inviting me.'

Iris bowed her head graciously. 'You're welcome. What Mark wants, Mark gets.'

She said this with a smile, but it was followed by a pregnant, punctuated silence. Mark was hidden behind a menu and said nothing. Poppy followed his lead and again scanned the barely comprehensible list of options, desperately searching for something she understood.

By the time she was halfway through the main course, Poppy was clear on one thing: the restaurant's lasagne was definitely not as good as her mother's. It was, however, an Italian word that she understood, making it one of four dishes she had been able to choose from without having to ask its meaning.

Iris and Mark chatted about life in Toronto, but everything they said was stunted and book-ended by silences that could have rivalled the ones Poppy and Clyde had held long ago. Poppy had to remind herself that it was only a year ago she'd been at their wedding, when they'd been full of smiles and in-jokes. Now they were as frosty as Poppy had previously believed Canada to be.

Mark was busy forking at his pasta when his phone started to ring. He glanced sideways at his wife, whose eyes were full of fire as she put her fork down calmly. She said nothing, but Poppy didn't need to be telepathic to know she was silently ordering Mark not to answer it.

As he held up a finger, Mark stood, retreating towards the back of the restaurant, phone to his ear. Poppy and Iris were left alone, on opposite sides of the circular table. They'd each eaten only half their meals, but Iris left her fork on the table as she wiped her mouth with a napkin.

'It's been really nice seeing you again,' she said.

'Um... Thanks,' Poppy replied, unsure what was going on.

Iris slipped her chair backwards and stood. 'I forgot to say so earlier but happy birthday. I hope you enjoy the rest of the evening.'

'Thank you...'

Iris slid the chair back underneath the table, picked up her bag and then strode towards the exit. Without another word, she had gone through the door, dress swishing behind her.

Poppy thought about trailing after her, but the reason for the absence of Iris's name in the online conversations with Mark was becoming apparent. And even if Poppy did race after Iris, what would she say? They barely knew one another. This conversation over dinner had been the first words they'd exchanged since the wedding.

Mark returned shortly after, brow crumpled in confusion, phone still in his hand. 'Where's Iris?' he asked.

Poppy nodded at the door. 'I think she left.'

Mark turned between Poppy and the exit. He sat, then stood, then sat again. Eventually he decided to stand. 'Sorry about this,' he said, striding towards the door and disappearing through it.

Poppy sipped her wine, unsure what to do. She couldn't exactly follow them, else she'd leave behind an upset restaurant owner wanting his money. She also didn't want to get left by herself, lumbered with the bill. With few other options, Poppy continued eating.

The door opened at regular intervals over the next ten minutes, and Poppy looked up each time – but it was never Mark. When the waiter returned to clear her bowl, she offered an apologetic shrug, saying he should leave Mark and Iris's plates. He gave her a semi-sympathetic look of someone who'd seen it all before. Probably worse, too.

Fifteen minutes after he'd left, Mark finally returned, hair windswept, face drained of colour. He gulped and sat, picking up his fork. 'Iris isn't feeling very well,' he said, shovelling in a mouthful of cold pasta.

Poppy's only reply was to sip her wine.

'That's a lie, obviously,' Mark added, putting his fork down again.

He glanced up, fixing Poppy with a look she'd never seen before. He seemed shattered, older than he was, cheeks sunken as he sucked them in. The excitement she'd seen when he was giving her a tour of the city earlier had long gone. He was broken.

'I'm going to have to go after her,' he said.

'What happened? You were so happy a year ago.'

Mark held his hands up. 'Toronto happened. Iris isn't a big-city girl. She misses her mum and her family. She was fed up in Manchester and missed Whitby – now she misses it even more. Her visa has been held up and might never get accepted, so she can't work. She doesn't have her own money and doesn't like taking what she calls "hand-outs". Then, because she's not working, she doesn't know how to meet anyone new.'

He sighed and ran a hand across the top of his head.

'It's not her fault, Pops.'

'I never said it was.'

'She's lonely and I don't know what to do about it. I came here to work and the hours are crazy. I *have* to go into the office and answer my phone when it rings. I *need* to reply to emails. That's the culture. She says I'm putting work before her and she's right – but I can't fix it. I have to choose between her and the job. Her and the city.'

Mark let out a long breath and stared off towards the back of the restaurant with glassy eyes. 'I think I've already lost her, Pops. She's been talking about going home. Her parents have said they will pay.'

Poppy bit her lip, not knowing what to say. She reached across the table and put her hand on top of his. 'If you love her, you should find a way to fix it. That might mean going home. There are always other jobs. There aren't always other people who love you.'

Mark nodded sadly, then looked up and caught her eye. His stare was so intense that Poppy had to turn away. Sometimes it really felt like he could read her mind.

He put her usual rectangular present on the table, along with his credit card. 'I wrapped that myself,' he said. 'I got it in this amazing little art shop on King Street. I left the business card inside so you can check it out for yourself. Eat and drink whatever you want, and then put it on my card. I'll call you tomorrow.'

'OK.'

'I'm sorry I've spoiled your birthday.'

Poppy stroked the back of his hand, thinking of what Neil had told her. She was the glue among the chaos and carnage of the soap opera that surrounded her.

'You haven't,' she replied.

Twenty-Four

Freya leaned back against the sofa in Poppy's flat, pushing her bloated abdomen upwards. Her skin was taut and riddled with thin purple stretch marks, while her belly button rested on top, like a flattened cherry.

'I've had enough of being pregnant,' she said as she ran her hands across her stomach.

Poppy glanced across at her and tried not to smile. Freya had let her hair grow out and it was as frizzy and long as it had ever been. She sipped from the cup of tea on the floor next to her and then flipped pages in the magazine she wasn't reading.

'What?' Freya said, catching Poppy's gaze.

'Do I really have to say it?'

Freya's lips cracked into a grin. 'All right, Pops, I get it. It takes two to tango. I'm a single mum who's about to be a double single mum. I still don't care what anyone thinks. Angie's gonna be a model one day – just look at her.'

Poppy prodded a large red Duplo brick across the floor towards Freya's daughter. Although she wasn't even a year old, Angela was utterly beautiful. Some children grew into their looks. Grumpy frowns and dumpy potato faces blossomed into angelic toddlers. Some kids were left with dumpy potato faces, not that a person could ever say as much to the child's parents. It was like a reflex: a parent said how gorgeous their child was, and the other person agreed. Poppy needed no such reflex with Angela. She'd inherited the darkness of her mother's skin with the cheekbones that presumably came from her father.

Angela pulled herself along the carpet and picked up the plastic brick. She turned it over, put it in her mouth, and then threw it away. Poppy picked it up again, wiping the saliva on her skirt, and then she flicked the brick in the direction of the radiator. Angela immediately set off after it, like a dog chasing a stick.

It was easy, Poppy thought, this parenting lark.

'Fast, ain't she?' Freya said proudly.

'If she doesn't make it as a model, she could be an athlete.'

'You saying she's not pretty enough to be a model?'

'No, I—' Poppy turned to see Freya grinning.

'Gotcha,' Freya said.

Angela had retrieved the brick and again started chewing the corner before deciding that it wasn't food. She tossed it back to Poppy and waited expectantly.

Poppy under-armed the piece of plastic in the opposite direction. 'So the council have sorted you out?' she asked.

'They're giving me a two-bed,' Freya replied. 'It's small though, so I'm still on to them, seeing if they can put me in something bigger.' She flipped another page of her magazine. 'Kids are the *best* thing, Pops.'

Poppy nodded but said nothing. From university, to various boys, to her job, to kids, there was always a new best thing with Freya. It was hard to argue that Angela was anything other than perfect, though. That said, Angela seemed determined to dispel this thought as she gurgled her appreciation and then dribbled a bit of orangey-pink vomit onto the floor, before promptly mashing it into the carpet with her hand.

'Aww, Pops, can you sort that?' Freya held her hands out, indicating her midriff. 'I'm sort of stuck here.'

Poppy rolled her eyes but didn't protest. With wipes already on standby, she dabbed the sick away from Angela's chin and top and then set to work on the carpet.

'Are you sure you're going to be all right with her?' Freya asked.

'What could possibly go wrong?' Poppy replied.

'She likes pulling stuff. Cushions, clothes, shoelaces: you name it.'

'Where are you off to today?'

Freya grimaced and wriggled on the carpet. 'Someone posted online last night that the Scope shop in town had a bunch of clothes dropped off. Proper stuff, too – labels and all that. I'm going to have a nosey through that, then the Oxfam shop always gets comics in at this time of the month. You can make a fortune if you find the right stuff.' She nodded at a pair of crammed bags-for-life next to the door. 'I've gotta go to the post office as well. You got anything that needs to go out?'

Poppy shook her head. 'Not today.'

Freya rolled onto her side and then used the arm of the sofa to heave herself up. She stretched and groaned, almost kicking over the remains of her tea. 'I might as well get off then,' she said.

Poppy lifted up Angela for her mum to give her a quick kiss and then they had a brief hug, before Freya waddled towards the door. 'I hate standing up,' she said.

Freya had only been gone for five minutes when the doorbell sounded. Poppy assumed her friend had forgotten something, so she lifted Angela onto her shoulder, propping her up one-handed, while opening the door with the other. Her eyes widened as she saw who it actually was on the other side.

'Dad…?' she said.

Poppy's father took a half-step back, almost standing on Madeleine. His gaze switched quickly from Poppy to Angela. 'Pops?'

Poppy hoisted the baby higher. 'This is Freya's daughter, Angela. Remember?'

Angela squirmed at the sound of her name, so Poppy returned her to the floor, where she promptly scarpered towards a giant teddy bear, which she wrestled to the floor.

Poppy welcomed her father and stepmother into the flat, where they found a spot on the sofa. Madeleine gently slapped Poppy's dad on the arm, giving him The Look. Poppy had given her father that look plenty of times in the past herself.

'What?' he protested.

'You know what,' his wife replied.

He hadn't asked about Angela's father – but Poppy and Madeleine both knew he'd been thinking it.

It had taken Poppy a little while to get used to thinking of Madeleine as her stepmum but their relationship was good enough. Poppy suppressed a smile and exchanged the briefest of knowing looks with the other woman.

Madeleine was a few years younger than Poppy's father, with dyed light blonde hair that was permanently bundled on top of her head. She pointed at the row of mounted photographs leaning against the wall in the corner.

'Did you draw those?' she asked.

'I take photos of my commissions,' Poppy replied. 'It's all one-of-a-kind stuff but I like to keep a record of everything.'

Madeleine crossed the room, picking up the first image and then flipping through the others. Poppy's father was wriggling on the sofa, wincing as he tried to get comfortable.

'You all right?' Poppy asked.

Her dad grunted something that might have been 'yes' but continued fidgeting.

'Your father won't go to the doctor,' Madeleine said without turning.

Poppy's dad rolled his eyes and shook his head. 'If I needed to visit the doctor, I'd do so.'

Poppy picked up Angela and manoeuvred her away from the electrical sockets. She gave her a cushion to play with instead and was met with an appreciative, dribbly gurgle.

Madeleine turned to look at Poppy. 'He says it's heartburn—'

'It *is* heartburn.'

'Heartburn doesn't last for weeks at a time.'

Madeleine and Poppy's father frowned at one another but there was no real malice between them. Poppy's father pushed himself up from the sofa. 'I'm old, Maddy. This is what happens when someone gets old. Now, if you'll excuse me, here is another thing that happens when you get old…' He disappeared through the living room door and then the toilet door closed along the hallway.

Angela threw the cushion away and turned to Poppy. She puffed her lips out with a babbling sloppy fart, which was the noise she always made when she wanted Poppy's attention. Somehow she'd mistaken the name 'Poppy' for 'wet fart'.

Poppy offered her index finger and Angela gripped it hard, trying to pull herself up.

'They're lovely at that age,' Madeleine said.

'They're *more* lovely when you give them back.'

Madeleine giggled. 'While your father's out of the room, there's something I wanted to ask. Will you do a portrait for us for our anniversary? I mentioned it to your father, but he didn't want to ask, and then—'

'Of course I will.'

'I'll pay, obviously.'

'It's fine. I don't want the money.'

Madeleine touched Poppy's arm in appreciation. 'There's one more thing,' she added, lowering her voice. 'Do you know any way to get him to the doctor?'

Poppy saw the concern in her face. 'Is it *that* bad?'

'I don't know. You know what he's like. He hides whatever it is but I'll catch him grimacing now and then. He also has problems sitting and standing. Perhaps it *is* age? He won't talk about it.'

'He's always been stubborn about things like that. I don't know what to tell you.'

'I'll keep nagging him.'

'Good luck with that.'

They locked eyes and both smiled in silent acknowledgement of shared experiences.

Madeleine put down the pictures and returned to the sofa. 'I've never had the opportunity to thank you,' she said.

'For what?'

'When your father and I got into this, we were both in an awkward position. I thought you might be jealous, believing that I was trying to take him away from you, or replace your mother. Your father said it would be fine but you never know.'

'I just want him to be happy.'

Madeleine nodded. 'Me too.'

They were interrupted by the flushing of the toilet and doors opening as Poppy's father blustered his way into the room. He stopped and stared between the two women. 'Were you two talking about me?'

Poppy broke into a grin. 'I bet you think this song is about you, eh Dad?'

He eyed her suspiciously and then sat next to Madeleine. She removed an A4 brown envelope from her bag and passed it to him.

'As well as coming to say happy birthday, we do have a second reason for being here,' he said.

'That sounds ominous.'

'Perhaps,' he replied, passing over the envelope. It wasn't sealed at the top and Poppy pulled out a few sheets of paper. She scanned the top page and then flicked through the rest, eyes darting from page to page as she moved quicker and quicker.

She looked up at her father and Madeleine, confused. 'These are the deeds to your house,' she said.

'Actually,' her father replied, 'they're the deeds to *your* house. They're all on the computers nowadays but we managed to get something printed out. Happy birthday.'

Poppy stared at the front page again, batting away Angela, who was trying to dribble on it.

'Why?' she asked.

Poppy's dad took Madeleine's hand. 'Because you're my number one, Pops. I love Maddy – but that house was always going to be yours. Maddy's got her own place anyway and I didn't want there to be any confusion down the line. It's my sixtieth this year and I decided now is the time.'

Madeleine was smiling wider than Poppy's father.

'I don't understand,' Poppy said. 'You've signed the house over to me?'

He shrugged. 'You have to sign the papers, but yes.'

She broke into a grin. 'So I can evict you?'

A hint of a smile wafted across his face. 'My solicitor wanted a clause to say that I was allowed to live there as long as I wanted but I had it removed. *Technically*, I'm your tenant who is living rent-free – but I decided we're all adults here…'

Poppy again read the top few lines, before moving the papers onto the side, away from Angela's groping hands.

'This is too much, Dad. I can't take this.'

He shook his head. 'If anything, Pops, it's not a real present. It would have been yours anyway. I've just brought everything forward by a few years.'

Poppy wasn't sure what to say, and then she realised something. 'Hang on, if this isn't my *actual* present, then you still owe me a real birthday present.'

She held out an expectant hand but got only a grin in return. Her father waved her across for a hug and kiss on the forehead.

When Poppy returned to the floor, Angela was busy bashing a selection of Duplo blocks together.

'What are you doing for your birthday?' Madeleine asked.

Poppy shrugged. 'Not much. I'm too old for big nights now.'

'You're twenty-four.'

'Exactly! Frey's pregnant, so she can't do much. We were thinking about the cinema but she needs to wee every half-hour. We'll probably stay in and watch a film. I might go for a walk first.'

'Where will you go?'

'Leigh Woods is only a couple of miles away. Sometimes I go out there to draw. Nobody bothers you.'

Poppy was about to add something else when there was the too-familiar sound of Angela burping. She turned to see a new blob of orange-pink gunge on the floor.

'It's a good job I'm going to have an entire house to my name,' Poppy said. 'There is no chance I'm getting the security deposit back on this place.'

My dearest Poppy,

I figure I've put it off long enough – so now it is time for the story of you, Poppy Kinsey.

At long last, I was pregnant. Much like your early teenage self, you were late from the very beginning. You were due on July the 20th and by then, I was huge. HUGE. Like a small van. It was a really warm summer and I felt horrible. I was sweaty all the time and couldn't keep myself cool. I'd take cold showers to try to get my body temperature down, but it made little difference.

July the 20th came and went. So did the 21st. And the 22nd. And so on. Your father would drive me around, swerving into potholes and going up and down Purley Hill in an attempt to send me into labour.

Still you didn't come.

We had curries: violent, tongue-burning, ear-popping, nose-running curries.

Still you didn't come.

Your father leapt out at me as I was coming out of the shower and I was so scared that I jumped backwards, slipped, landed on the toilet seat and accidentally kicked him somewhere he didn't appreciate. (In his version, there was no 'accident' about it – but that's my story and I'm sticking to it.)

Still you didn't come.

We tried everything we could think of but you were happy where you were.

It got to July 31st and, to be honest, I was sick of being pregnant. Your father was unavoidably working away which was, of course, the signal for my contractions to begin. Typical! Time-keeping, young lady!

All was in hand, though, because we'd already arranged for Mr Ashcroft, who lived across the road, to drive me to Ledford Hospital if this occurred. While that was happening, Mrs Ashcroft would call the office to which your father was heading and leave him a message.

Easy, right?

Well, no.

We were on this country lane about a quarter of the way to Ledford when Mr Ashcroft's car died. There was no slowing down, no sputters, it just rolled to a stop. The electrics had cut out and it was stone-cold dead. This was still a little before mobiles became widespread, so neither of us had any way to let anyone know. We ended up waiting on the side of the road for another vehicle to come by. I was holding onto the top of Mr Ashford's car and having contractions every six or seven minutes.

It wasn't exactly how I'd pictured having my first child.

Luckily, a bus turned up on its way to Ledford. Of course, I'd forgotten my purse and Mr Ashcroft only had a twenty-pound note on him, which the driver wouldn't take because he couldn't make change. They were haggling back and forth, which was a good time for another contraction to make itself known. The driver took a look at me, told me to sit down, and then floored it.

'Brilliant,' you might be thinking. 'We're off to the hospital.' Well, yes – but then my waters broke. The driver looked petrified, which was unsurprising. My waters were swilling on the floor around his cabin, like a river that had burst its banks. He was so out of his depth that he was hurtling past bus stops where people were waiting. I saw people shaking their fists as he drove past them without

stopping. Then, of course, there were other passengers who must've thought they'd been kidnapped. Somehow, nobody complained.

Things were going about as well as possible when we reached the dual carriageway heading into Ledford. Apparently, a lorry had jack-knifed, with traffic backed up for about three miles. People had stopped and got out of their cars. Nobody was going anywhere. It was hot, I was sweating, and I was contracting every three or four minutes at this point. I'm not sure who was more scared: me, the kidnapped passengers, Mr Ashcroft, or the bus driver.

After a few minutes of hearing me scream, the driver must've decided enough was enough because he got on his radio to the bus depot. Shortly after, the traffic started to part on the other side of the road. At first I didn't know why, but then I heard the sirens and saw the lights. A police car emerged and crossed the carriageway. It stopped in front of the bus and then two officers got out. They came to the bus doors and climbed inside, standing in my water, of course. They looked at the driver, looked at me, looked where they were standing, and then they got on their radios.

Before I knew it, the bus was getting a police escort through the traffic to the hospital. I have no idea why they didn't just put me in their car. Perhaps they'd actually responded to kidnap reports from the other passengers. Amazing, right? Even back then, you were causing chaos.

I got to the hospital and everything was finally going well. I was in the delivery ward and there were doctors, nurses, midwives, police officers, bus drivers, Mr Ashcroft, and who knows who else. You name a person and they were probably at your birth.

The problem was that your father wasn't there. As helpful as Mr Ashcroft had been, I really didn't want a sixty-something neighbour standing there as my first child arrived.

Of course, I couldn't express that like a normal person because my contractions were coming thick and fast. The midwife was telling me not to panic, which only made me panic more. It was this big festival of panicking and sweating and screaming and it was awful.

Then the door opened, and it was your dad.

He'd dumped the car on the dual carriageway and run three miles to the hospital, bad back and all. I'd never known him run but he must have really gone for it. He was a mess – dripping with sweat and looking like he'd drowned – but it was like everything was suddenly in place.

Which is why I presume you then decided to make your first appearance. You screamed your way into the world and everything was wonderful. I remember this particular moment, a few seconds before the doctors returned. It was your father, me and you – the three of us alone in this hospital room.

And it was beautiful, Pops. The greatest moment of my life. Amid the disarray and confusion, the worry and stress, there were these few seconds of perfection. In those seconds, I suppose I learned that chaos doesn't need to breed more chaos. Sometimes all it takes is the right person by your side to make everything all right in the end.

Your father looked at me, then he looked at you, then he looked at me again and he said: 'We nailed it, didn't we?'

I frowned at him and said: '"Nailed it?" Where did that come from?' But he laughed and so I laughed – and then you made this little gurgling sound, like you were laughing too because Daddy was such a silly softy.

As sentences go, it was pretty stupid but I suppose, after all this time, I have to admit he was right. Because we did. We absolutely nailed it, because we got you.

Then, of course, we had to decide what to name you. But you already know that story.

Happy birthday,
Mum

Poppy emerged from the park and turned towards Clifton Suspension Bridge. A pair of cyclists zipped along the path next to her, while a car gave way to a vehicle coming from the opposite direction. She continued past the low red-brick wall until she reached the taller, far more imposing white fence of the bridge itself. Strings of wire stretched across the top, but the ugliness didn't detract from the sheer wonder of the view below. Poppy always felt a little nervous as she gazed over Avon Gorge. On one side of the river, a forest of puffy green trees grew into one another; on the other, a mass of buildings stretched back to the city. Through the middle, the water snaked into the distance. Poppy's eyes goggled at the height, though it was nothing compared to where she'd been standing a year previously.

As she neared the centre of the bridge, Poppy stopped to hold onto the fence and stare at the valley below. She'd made this journey numerous times in the past to get from the city to the woods, but never ceased to be struck by both the natural beauty of the gorge, and the achievement of the bridge that had been built over it.

Small groups of people were stopping to take photographs as they crossed, while cars continued to skim past behind.

Poppy took out her phone but there were no new messages, so she turned it off, not wanting to be disturbed. It was a warm evening, the sun peeping through the wash of fluffy clouds. She wanted to find a spot on the edge of the woods and look for something to draw. It wasn't the rock and roll birthday she might have wanted in years gone by, but it would do for her now.

She was about to continue across the bridge when she noticed a lad standing close to the barrier, staring out towards the river below. He was by himself, seventeen or eighteen, with neatly parted black hair, jeans and an ill-fitting black hoody with a skull on the front. As she watched, he pressed a palm to the metal barrier and took a deep breath.

'Hello,' Poppy said, moving a couple of steps closer to him.

He jolted as she spoke, blinking rapidly as he turned to face her. He muttered something she didn't catch and then turned back to the fence.

'Are you all right?' Poppy asked.

'Yeah.'

'What are you doing?'

He removed his hand from the metal. 'Nothing.'

Poppy turned from him to the drop below. He seemed twitchy, unsure of himself. 'Are you sure everything's all right?' she asked.

The teenager took a small step back from the fence. He glanced quickly between Poppy and the gorge. 'I'm fine.'

His eyes flicked back and forth between Poppy and the gorge again. He settled on Poppy. 'Who are you?' he asked.

'No one – I was out for a walk and you looked like you might've been thinking… things.'

His eyes flicked once more before he again settled on Poppy, Adam's apple bobbing. 'What things?'

She shrugged. Shivered. Tried to make eye contact. 'I don't know.'

He shook his head. 'I'm out for a walk, too.'

'Nice area, isn't it?'

He turned in a semicircle, still only a step from the fence. 'I s'pose.'

Poppy waited until he caught her eye and then she wouldn't let him go. 'It's all right, y'know?'

He nodded quickly. 'Yeah…'

'I was higher than this a year ago: way, way up in the sky. A bit pissed off, annoyed at other people, more annoyed at myself.'

The lad's eyes narrowed but he took another small step away from the fence. A couple passed hand-in-hand on the path behind him, oblivious to what was going on. The woman apologised, even though there was no need. The teenager turned from her to Poppy, not peering down at the gorge this time.

'What were you annoyed about?' he asked.

'Nothing really – stupid stuff. Falling out with friends. Stuck going nowhere. The usual.'

'What happened?'

'I ended up talking to this Australian lad.'

'What did he say?'

'Not much – he asked if I was all right, if I wanted to tell him my problems…'

'Oh.'

Poppy turned to the river. She felt it rushing towards her, but blinked the sensation away. 'I'm going to carry on my walk,' she said, nodding past him. 'I was going that way. OK?'

He pointed in the opposite direction. 'I was going that way.'

'You should keep going.'

He gulped and nodded quickly. 'Right.'

With that, he pulled up the hoody and drooped his head. He moved quickly past her, hurrying along the path, off the end of the bridge and into the park, disappearing behind a tree. Poppy watched him go and then hoisted her bag higher on her shoulder, not entirely sure what had just happened.

Twenty-Five

Purley had been blessed by the day of all days. The green was the greenest Poppy had ever seen it, amplified by the sun cascading from the most perfect of blue skies. Stalls lined both sides of the cobbled streets that encircled the green, with rainbow streamers looped from building to building. A smattering of locals were putting the finishing touches to various stalls, but it was unnervingly quiet given how busy everything would be by lunchtime.

Poppy emerged from the corner shop and pressed the pint of milk she'd bought to her forehead. The cool condensation dribbled from the glass bottle, working its magic so quickly that she shivered, despite the heat. Glass milk bottles had seemingly disappeared from everywhere except this corner of the world and Poppy had a pang of nostalgia as she removed the silver lid and sipped the cream from the top.

She was close to the bottom of Purley Hill when she spotted Madeleine coming towards her from the other side of the bridge. Madeleine was walking quickly, bonnet over her head, canvas bag-for-life over her shoulder. She noticed Poppy a moment after Poppy saw her, and stopped on the spot. She opened her arms and they embraced before Poppy turned towards the green.

'Happy birthday,' Madeleine said. 'I didn't know what time you'd be getting down.'

'I caught the bus last night,' Poppy replied. 'Freya and I are staying at Dad's house.'

'*Your* house.'

'My house,' Poppy agreed, although it didn't sound right.

Madeleine nodded towards the green. 'Bit different, isn't it? The parish council have been planning this for ages. Who'd have thought someone founded this place 1,500 years ago?'

'It looks like it's going to be some party.'

Madeleine nodded. 'Well, as much of a party as you can get when there's a stall set up solely to sell home-made jam.'

Poppy laughed, switching the milk bottle from one hand to the other before she caught the look on Madeleine's face. The other woman was staring towards the green, bottom lip trembling. 'Your father would have loved today,' she whispered.

Any reply she might have had was stuck at the back of Poppy's throat as she looked past Madeleine towards the hill.

'Sorry,' Madeleine added.

Poppy shook her head, wanting to say it was fine but not able to form the words. Madeleine knew what she meant, cupping Poppy's shoulder comfortingly. 'I've told you this before – and I know I'm not your mum or dad – but I'm here if you ever need someone to talk to. You've got my number and you know where I am.'

'Thank you,' Poppy croaked, gripping Madeleine's hand quickly and then letting her go.

The two women stared at each other for the briefest of moments because that was all they needed. The words had already been spoken too many times over recent months.

Madeleine was blinking rapidly. 'I'm sure I'll see you later but, if not, I hope you enjoy the day. Don't eat too much.'

Poppy managed a humourless laugh. 'I won't.'

'Actually, eat what you want. I had a sneak peak of Mrs Rawtenstall's home-made fairy cakes yesterday and they were outstanding, even by her standards.'

'I'll make sure I give them a go.'

There was an awkward moment, with neither of them quite knowing how to say goodbye. In the end, Madeleine offered a short nod and then they headed in opposite directions.

Poppy started towards the hill and then took the path that ran alongside the river, heading towards her dad's house.

Her house.

She walked slowly, watching a pair of small ducks flap and quack at one another before they settled in a shaded spot underneath the bridge. Watching them, Poppy did a double-take as she spotted a pair of girls sitting in the alcove underneath the brickwork of the bridge arch. They were fourteen or fifteen: all short skirts, big hair and too much make-up. Poppy listened for a few moments, only catching snippets of their conversation – boys' names, 'mum', 'dad', 'Purley', 'stupid' – but it was enough. Roll back a decade or so and it could have been her and Freya in the same spot, agonising over things that now seemed incomprehensibly unimportant.

The teenagers had been passing a bag of crisps between them and one of them now flicked the empty packet into the river. It caught on a rock and the ripples grabbed it, dragging the packet towards the village centre.

As it swirled into the distance, one of the girls noticed Poppy and matched her stare with a fearless, silent challenge to say something if she dared. Poppy well knew that look – she'd seen Freya give plenty of them when they'd been that age.

Had she really got to the point in her life where she scolded teenagers for being, well, teenagers?

Not today.

Poppy shrugged and continued along the trail, sipping the milk until it was half gone and she was at the end of her path.

The house was cool and quiet inside. On the fridge, Freya had arranged the magnetic letters to spell a four-digit, simple-to-understand message.

BRB – F

Poppy filled the kettle and clicked it on, then sat at the kitchen table. Aside from the gentle fizzing of the water being heated, the house was silent.

From nowhere, there was a lump in Poppy's throat and tears stinging the corners of her eyes. Since everything had happened with her father at the start of the year, Poppy had continued to live in Bristol, despite owning this four-bedroom house. This was the first time she'd been here by herself since he'd died. No mum, no dad, no Madeleine. Just her.

When Poppy and Freya had arrived late the night before, they'd gone straight to bed. Now, Poppy entered the living room to see nothing had been moved since the funeral. Madeleine had been popping in regularly to make sure everything was still in order.

A thin layer of dust was clinging to the furniture, with a red standby light burning accusingly on the front of the television.

Poppy turned in a circle, taking everything in. She wondered if she wanted to keep it, or to get rid of everything and start again. When she spotted her father's bureau in the back corner of the room, Poppy crossed to it, running her fingers across the smooth grain of the varnished wood. She could remember him sitting here in years gone by, writing letters before it went out of fashion. The key was sitting on top, as if it had been left out specifically for her.

Perhaps it had?

Poppy picked it up, about to unlock the cabinet, when another thought occurred to her. She pushed the chair out of the way and then lay on the carpet, wriggling and shuffling until she was directly underneath the bureau. It was dusty and murky in the shadowed back corner but through it all, Poppy could make out the scrawled crayon self-portrait she had drawn many years previously. Her face was a blobby circle, eyes enormous and taking up half her face. Her hair was straight lines jutting off at every angle, with the image topped by an enormous ear-to-ear grin.

As self-portraits went, it wasn't the most flattering, but looking at it, Poppy found herself gulping back more tears. Underneath the drawing was a simple message written in crayon, which she had forgotten about:

'I love my mummy + daddy'

Poppy slid back out and then sat on the chair and unlocked the cabinet. Waiting at the front was the final envelope with her name on the front. In previous years, her father had always made sure that she had the envelope by her birthday. This year, he'd had no such chance.

The envelope was as beautifully textured as the others. Poppy ran her fingers across the front, knowing that this was it. Once she'd read this letter, there would be no more contact from her parents, only memories. Each year, Poppy had agonised over whether she wanted to read the contents of the letter, but she'd always been relieved to in the end.

Over time, the image of her mother had started to fade. The curves of her face, the shape of her eyebrows, the way her hair had looked when it was down. Little things. Her letters didn't make the physical memory any stronger, but they did remind Poppy of the person her mother once was.

As soon as she flicked apart the bow and opened the envelope to read the contents, Poppy was left grinning. It wasn't the message she'd expected from her mum – it was far, far better. She stared at the page and then turned it over, taking in its meaning and knowing her mother was right. As final words went, they were pretty good.

Poppy folded the letter back into the envelope and locked the cabinet but, before she could do anything else, the doorbell chimed. It was a traditional *ding-dong*, the sound of Poppy's childhood as either Mark, Freya, or both had called round to see if she was going out.

The final note echoed around the hallway as Poppy opened the door, to be met by a pairing she hadn't seen together in a very long time.

It was a step back into the past, into memories Poppy had thought she'd forgotten, and to an image she hadn't thought she'd ever see again. Freya and Mark, together. There was a moment in which it felt like she'd been punched, her chest tight, breath seemingly far away.

Freya was cradling Angelina on one shoulder while, next to her, Mark was holding a wriggling Angela with one arm and clasping a heavy-looking canvas bag in the other.

Poppy looked between them and then burst out laughing as she nodded at Mark.

'Are you still carrying around her stuff after all these years?'

Mark gasped a wearied sigh as he placed Angela gently on the floor of Poppy's hallway. She instantly shot past Poppy into the house with a splutter of something that might have been 'Poppy' but sounded more like 'Pooey'.

'What are you doing here?' Poppy asked.

Mark held both hands up. 'Why do you think? Purley's fifteen-hundredth birthday.'

She turned to Freya. 'Yes, but why are you *both* here?'

Freya turned to Mark and shrugged. 'I took the girls out for a walk and found him hanging around the public toilets—'

'I wasn't hanging around, I'd been—'

She grinned. 'He was hanging around and I thought he might get arrested. Anyway, I told him I was staying at your house. He kidnapped Angela and here we are.'

'That's not exactly how it happened,' Mark insisted.

He didn't have an opportunity to expand as there was the sound of something crashing behind them. The three of them dashed through to the living room, Poppy's heart thundering as she expected to find Angela had somehow pulled the TV off the wall. There'd be shattered glass all around.

Angela was actually sitting among a pile of Duplo bricks that she'd yanked off the sofa. She sat surrounded by plastic squares, thwacking one into another until they clicked together. She held up the results.

'Dog,' she said.

Freya placed Angelina on the ground and she was instantly off, too, wriggling in the direction of the back door.

'Dog,' Angela repeated.

'That's not a dog, sweetie,' Freya replied.

'Dog.'

Mark had managed to get between Angelina and the door but that only meant she was now trying to lick his shoes. Either that or eat them. 'Is it always like this?' he asked.

Poppy nodded. 'It's usually noisier.'

By the time Poppy, Freya and Mark made it to the green later in the afternoon, the centre of Purley was bouncing to the sounds of Status Quo. Presumably someone on the parish council had hijacked the sound system because 'Rockin' All Over The World' was seeping from the speakers as if it was the village's official theme tune. Not only had the entire village turned out, but hundreds of visitors, perhaps even thousands, had streamed in from the surrounding communities.

The stalls were doing a roaring trade in jam, cakes and various bric-a-brac, while the Mr Whippy vans close to the cemetery were doing one hell of a lot of whipping. Even more crucial than that, the only pub in the village had a pop-up stall on the edge of the green selling cider and lager. Quite how they'd got that past the council, Poppy wasn't sure – but she wasn't complaining.

Poppy sipped her cider and stretched her legs out on the grass, enjoying the prickle of the sun on her skin. All around her, other couples and groups were doing the same. Chatting, smiling and drinking.

'They should do this every year,' Mark said. He was in a tight-fitting vest with shorts to his knees and a tan that would more normally be associated with someone who lived on a Mediterranean beach.

'It's not quite the same if they have a fifteen-hundred-and-first birthday party,' Poppy replied.

'You know what I mean.'

'I do indeed.'

Mark nodded towards the edge of the green, where Freya was pushing her daughters in a pushchair. Angelina looked almost identical to how Angela had at her age. By the time they were both a little older, they'd be easily mistaken for twins.

'Why did she call one Angela and one Angelina?' he asked.

'I don't ask too many questions like that,' Poppy replied. 'You know what Freya's like. The next one will probably be called Angelika or something like that. She'll be in the process of starting a family dynasty.'

'They're a right handful.'

'More than *one* handful.'

'Where's the dad?'

'*Dads*,' Poppy replied. 'That's another thing I don't get into. She's doing all right, though. Still running her eBay business and getting by. She's in her Bristol flat and seeing this lad named Jez.'

Mark nodded towards a couple walking along the edge of the green hand-in-hand. 'Hang on a minute. Is that Georgina and Ed? Didn't they hate each other at school?'

Poppy pushed herself up higher and squinted in the direction he'd indicated. She wasn't sure, but it did look like their old schoolmates. 'We could spend all day sitting here, spotting people we used to know,' she said.

'True.'

Mark had more of his drink and then rolled on his side to look at her. She'd not seen much of him in the best part of two years. He'd remained in Toronto after Iris had returned to England and Poppy hadn't asked too many questions about the end of their relationship. All she knew for sure was that they were divorced. She figured he'd tell her the details if he wanted. They'd messaged about other things

– movies, TV shows, music, food, city stuff – and then, six weeks before, he said he'd be moving back to England at some point in the near future. Poppy guessed this was the 'near future'.

Mark smiled with his lips together. There was still that twinkle. After all this time, it still felt like he knew her.

'There's something I need to tell you, Pops,' he said.

'Last time you said that, you were moving to Canada.'

'It's London this time. I'm going to be there permanently from next month. I applied for a job while I was still in Toronto and it's taken this long for things to go through.'

'Where are you living at the moment?'

He turned away, watching Freya again. 'I'm back with Mum and Dad.'

Poppy sat up. 'In Purley?'

'Right. Ten years, via Manchester, Whitby and Toronto and I'm back where I started.'

'Not really.'

'It feels like it. I swore the other day and Mum looked at me as if I'd just kicked a cat. I realised I'd never sworn in front of them before.'

Poppy ruffled his hair as he squirmed away. 'Aww, that's really cute,' she teased. 'You're still their little boy.'

She laughed and he joined in, before they lay back on the grass, ear to ear.

'I'm sorry I wasn't here for your dad, Pops…'

'It's not your fault.'

'It sounded like it was sudden?'

Poppy stared up at a puffy cloud drifting aimlessly over the village. For a fraction of a second, she could make out a face staring back at her and then it separated, each part floating in slightly different directions.

'Madeleine was great,' Poppy replied, not answering the question. 'Somehow I've ended up with the house and I don't know what to do with it.'

'Are you going to live in the village?'

'I don't think I could come back, not permanently. It feels too… small.' She paused. 'Does that sound really arrogant?'

'Some people marry the first person they lay eyes on, have a bunch of kids and spend their lives five minutes from where they grew up. Others go out and see the world. Who's to say any one side is more right than the other? Whatever makes you happy, right?'

'I guess.' Poppy paused again. 'I don't know if I'm going to sell it. I probably should, then get something somewhere else where I want to live. It's just… I grew up there. I can't imagine somebody else living there.'

'Only you can decide.'

Poppy breathed in the warm air, listening to the sounds of everyone around her. 'Life was easier when all you had to worry about was making sure you caught the last bus home on a Friday night,' she said. 'Now it's all house prices and legal documents.'

'We're getting old, Pops…'

Poppy was about to reply when something landed on her midriff. She shot up into a sitting position, gasping for breath as she realised it was Angela.

'Pooey!'

Freya stepped in front of the sun, casting a shadow across them as Poppy picked the child up.

'Sorry about that,' Freya said. 'I unstrapped her from the pushchair and she was off. She's definitely going to be an athlete when she's older. When she's not modelling, that is.'

Poppy was still struggling for breath, not wanting to point out that Angela could also be a rugby player given the frequency and ferocity of the way she ran at and hit things. No mother wanted to be told that their darling daughter might grow up to play rugby, however, so Poppy deposited the child back with Freya, who offered a token finger-wagging. Angela was only half paying attention, delving through Mark's canvas bag, which was full of a picnic. Freya ended up using the pushchair as an impromptu prison, clamping her daughter into place and pulling the straps tightly. Meanwhile, Angelina slept.

'I'm knackered, Pops,' Freya said as she collapsed onto the ground. She looked it, with sweat pooling on her top lip. Sunshine and Freya's hair never got on and this was no exception, with the heat making it expand to afro-like proportions. She wrenched a huge bundle of it backwards and then slipped a large rubber band around it.

'I'm not sure what you expect me to do,' Poppy replied.

'Fancy two kids for a week or so? Perhaps a fortnight? I'll come back eventually, promise.'

'I think I'm all right,' Poppy replied.

Freya nodded at Mark. 'You?'

'I'm fine, too.'

'I don't think you can put kids on eBay, either,' Freya said.

Freya spun as an older woman strode past, offering a disapproving stare before she turned away. 'I'm joking,' Freya called after her. There was no reply.

Mark removed a cake bar from his picnic bag and started to unwrap it. 'What are you doing for your birthday, Pops? Other than this?'

Poppy turned to face him, suddenly feeling hungry, even though she'd spent large parts of the afternoon eating. 'I've not thought about it.'

As she said it, a smile crept onto her face as an idea formed.

'What?' Freya asked.

Poppy pushed herself up onto her knees and surveyed the crowd. A barbecue had started up somewhere near the pub and meaty smoke was drifting across the green. 'I did see something earlier,' she said.

'What?'

She stood over her two friends. 'Can we go for a walk?'

Poppy didn't wait for their replies, walking slowly through the crowd and heading towards the row of stalls outside Mrs Dowson's Sweets. It didn't take long for Mark and Freya to catch her. Mark had his bag over his shoulder, with Freya using the pushchair as a battering ram to clear a path through the crowd.

'What are we doing?' Mark asked.

'You'll see.'

Poppy weaved her way along the first row of stalls, trying to remember where everything had been. She passed Mrs Rawtenstall's table of cakes, with Mrs Tunley's competing stall on the other side of the street – they were the Israel and Gaza of the cake world. She kept going until she was at the pub. The sickly smell of sweet scrumpy was on the breeze, sending Poppy back to her adolescence and days of drinking under the bridge.

She still wasn't quite sure where it was.

And then she saw it.

Poppy felt her excitement mounting as she reached the stall at the end of the row. There was a bare wooden table at the front with a string of multicoloured bunting across the top of two poles above. The man behind the stall was someone Poppy didn't recognise: probably a bloke who'd moved in recently because she'd have known him otherwise. More to the point, he'd have known her. He was fifty or sixty, with rugged silver stubble and a thick wad of nose hairs that Poppy thought must make it hard to breathe.

It looked like he was trying to sell the contents of a bin, with lines of battered ornaments spread across the table next to some old coins and postcards. Poppy, though, was more interested in the item resting against the front of the stall. 'How much for the bike?' she asked.

The man scratched his chin and then looked from Poppy to the bike, to Mark, to Freya, to the pushchair and then back at Poppy again. 'Hundred quid.'

Poppy coughed in surprise. This guy probably ran a sandwich shop in a service station, she thought, given his grasp on what things should cost. She pressed down on the back wheel. 'The tyres are nearly flat.'

'Ninety then.'

'The mudguards are rusty.'

The man stepped around to the front of the stall and poked at the brown mudguards. 'All right, eighty.'

'If I'm going to pay eighty quid for a bike, I want to have a test ride.'

His eyes narrowed. 'How do I know you won't nick it?'

'I'm not gonna nick it.'

'How do I know that?'

Poppy turned to Mark and Freya for support but their faces were blank with bemusement at the thought she might pay for this rust heap.

'How about I leave you something valuable?' Poppy said. 'When I return the bike, I get it back.'

He scratched his chin and then rearranged his crotch. 'All right,' he replied.

Poppy turned to Mark. 'Can I borrow your credit card?'

'Why mine?'

'Because he wants something valuable and mine… isn't.'

Mark's eyebrows met in the middle but he removed his card anyway and passed it across. The man scanned the digits – possibly memorising them – and then stuck it in his pocket.

'I'll be right back,' Poppy said, wheeling the bike towards the bottom of Purley Hill, Freya on one side, Mark on the other.

'What are you doing?' Mark asked when they were clear of the crowd.

'I'm going to push this bike up to the top of the hill, then I'm going to ride it all the way back down again.'

Poppy sensed her friends exchanging a 'has-she-gone-mad' look, but neither of them questioned her.

Getting to the top of the hill was harder than Poppy had imagined. Freya waited at the bottom, sensibly not wanting to shove the pushchair and her two children all the way to the top, only to come back down again. Mark didn't seem to mind, staying at Poppy's side as they trudged up and up.

'We're quite high,' he said as they neared the top.

'That's the point.'

'What's the point?'

'It's supposed to be scary.'

Mark glanced over his shoulder. 'That bike looks quite rickety.'

'I'm being spontaneous and it was all I had to hand.'

'You're not going to pay eighty quid for it, are you?'

'I wouldn't pay *eight* quid for it. I only need it for one thing.'

'What?'

Poppy pushed the bike to the brow of the hill and then spun it around. 'Gorgeous, isn't it?' she said.

'Purley?'

Poppy looked at the entire village laid out below her. The beautiful church, the green, the cobbled streets decked with stalls. Houses speckled out towards the expanse of fields in the distance. It would always be special to her.

'You don't appreciate it until you go somewhere else and then come back,' Poppy said. 'I don't think I could live here again, but it'll always be home to me.'

Mark said nothing at first but she knew he was thinking the same. 'It's so colourful,' he said, eventually. He spoke so softly that the breeze almost stole the words. With the added height of the hill, the wind was stronger here, flipping Poppy's hair back and forth.

He was right, Poppy thought. It was incredibly colourful. Even though the green was covered with people, there were bright patches of grass poking through the crowds. The streamers surrounding the cobbled square alternated from red to blue to yellow to green – and then there was the bright array of Union flags and various fancy dress costumes.

'Why are we up here?' Mark asked.

'For my mum.'

'Oh.'

Poppy lowered the saddle and straddled the bike. She had no helmet, not to mention the fact that the bike was a potential death trap.

Still…

She stared down at the dot of Freya far below. She offered a small wave that Poppy returned.

'You're crazy,' Mark said.

'Yes, I am.'

Poppy put her left foot on the pedal and pushed off with her right. The bike started to move so slowly that she momentarily thought she might topple off.

Then gravity took hold.

The frame rattled over the crust of gritty stones and holes as Poppy gripped the handlebars as tightly as she could. The wind was battering her face, so Poppy ducked lower, feeling her hair flap behind her. It took a few seconds before she realised she was enjoying it. She nudged the handlebars slightly to steer around a larger pothole and then righted the line so that she was in the middle of the empty road.

'Woooooo!'

The bottom of the hill was rushing towards her all too soon as Poppy shrieked a second cry of joy. It was only as her fingers started to clench the brakes that she realised she'd not tested them. A vision flashed across her mind of the bike hurtling past the bottom of the hill, flying over the bridge and embedding itself in Mrs Rawtenstall's cake stall. Cake was soft, wasn't it? It should provide a good cushion…

Poppy squeezed the brakes gently and felt the callipers grip the wheel rims. She slewed slightly right as she crested the bottom of the hill. A high-pitched squeak erupted from the stopping mechanism as she clasped the levers harder. People were turning to stare, wondering who the lunatic was, but the bike eventually squawked its way to a skidded stop.

Heart thumping, fingers shaking, Poppy climbed off the bike and turned to see Freya walking towards her.

'*That* was mental,' Freya said.

'Yes, it was.'

'Why'd you do it?'

Poppy shrugged. 'Because I might never get another chance.'

Freya stared at her for a few seconds and then held her phone up. 'I've gotta go, Pops. Jez is five minutes away and we're going back to Bristol.'

Mark was out of breath as he joined them on the other side of the bridge, having run down the hill. 'Are you all right?' he panted.

Freya eyed him sideways. 'Course I'm all right.'

'I meant Poppy.'

'Oh.'

Freya reached out a hand and tugged Mark towards her. She kissed him on the cheek and then whispered something in his ear. He stepped away, lips tight as he nodded.

'I've got to go,' Freya said, pointing past the church. 'I'm going that way, so I'll see ya when I see ya.'

She hugged Poppy and shunted the pushchair onto the green, before setting off for the other side.

'Can I get my credit card back now?' Mark asked.

The warmth of the afternoon turned into a balmy evening as Purley began to empty. Poppy and Mark strolled around the village, saying hello to familiar faces and convincing themselves that their metabolism was good enough to deal with the multiple pints of cider and conveyor belt of cakes they were consuming. The war between Mrs Tunley's cakes and Mrs Rawtenstall's was seemingly at an impasse as they had both sold out, with the street celebration turning out to be their Good Friday Agreement.

Poppy and Mark eventually started walking back to her house along the familiar path that followed the river. They'd only gone a short distance when something occurred to Poppy. She turned back to look at the alcove underneath the arch. The teenage girls had gone.

'Come with me,' Poppy said, leading Mark back the way they'd come. Moments later, they were sitting in their age-old space hidden under the bridge. They could hear the hum of villagers packing away their stalls, along with the gentle babble of the river. Otherwise, it was wonderfully peaceful. The brickwork was cold underneath Poppy's backside but there was something reassuringly familiar about the grooves scraping into her.

'It's probably nine or ten years since I last sat here,' Poppy said.

'A lot's happened,' Mark replied.

'Remember when Frey nicked that bottle of JD from her mum's house and we drank the lot down here…?'

'I remember the start of that afternoon – not so much the end.'

'My dad covered for us all. He picked us up, then phoned your mum and Frey's mum, saying you were staying at our house. You slept on the bathroom floor and I woke up in bed with Freya's feet in my face. Dad told me that was my one and only get-out-of-jail-free pass.'

Poppy rested her head against the bricks and closed her eyes.

'I've got your present,' Mark said.

She heard him digging through his bag and, when she opened her eyes, Mark was offering a small rectangle that was wrapped in polka dot paper. The corners were creased and messy. 'I *knew* you didn't wrap those presents in years gone by,' Poppy said.

'I did!'

Poppy pointed at the corners. '*This* is how a boy wraps.'

Mark's lips turned upwards. 'OK, I might have had a bit of help…'

Poppy laughed and threatened to poke him in the ribs, getting a joyous yelp in return. She twisted the gift in her hand, feeling the hardness of the contents. 'Thank you, but your presents are no longer valid,' she said. 'I *do* draw. It doesn't make much money, but I make enough to pay my bills. It's my job.'

'Open it, Pops.'

Poppy didn't need telling twice. It was still her birthday, after all. She ripped through the polka dots until she revealed… Something that wasn't pencils. It was a flat, plastic crimson box.

'What have you done?' she asked, suddenly nervous.

'Open it.'

Poppy did, clicking the box lid up until what was left of the sun snagged on the silvery sparkle of what was inside. She stared at the contents, not daring to touch.

'Where did you get this?' she breathed.

'I had pictures of you wearing your old necklace and this is the closest I could find. It's not exactly the same. I found it in a vintage jewellery shop in Toronto.'

Poppy removed the necklace from the box, running her fingers across the slim leaf shapes that were dotted around the chain. It might not have been her original, but it was close. Poppy twisted on the spot, holding the chain around her neck and letting Mark clip it into place.

'Thank you,' she said.

'Happy birthday.'

Poppy traced the outline of the leaves with her thumb in the way she used to with the original. They sat in silence for a few minutes, listening to the water, to the village.

It was Poppy who broke the hush. 'When Freya said goodbye to you, she whispered something in your ear…'

Mark said nothing, rearranging his bag and pretending he hadn't heard.

'Mark…?'

'What?'

'What did she say?'

He stopped rustling and turned to face the water. She saw his chest rise and fall and then he reached out and took her hand. Poppy felt chilled in the shadow but he was warm and his thumb brushed across the back of her hand. 'Not much.'

Neither of them spoke for a moment, with Poppy realising she had no right to ask. If Freya had wanted to be heard, she would have spoken louder. They might have grown up a trio, might have been two-plus-one for a while – but after all this time, they were very much three individuals.

'Do you want to go for a drink?' Mark asked. His voice was husky, the words almost sticking in his throat. Poppy turned to face him but he was staring at the water.

'I think we've drunk enough today,' she replied.

He shook his head. 'Not now, Pops. Not today. I'm asking if you want to go *for a drink* sometime. You and me.'

Poppy gazed at the side of his face, taking in his jawline and the cheekbones that, at one point, she could have drawn from memory with no guides at all.

She blinked.

She breathed.

Then she gave him her answer.

My dearest Poppy,

Every day begins with a blank page. Turn over: this is yours.

Happy birthday,

Mum

A Letter from Kerry

I can't remember where I came up with the initial pitch for *Ten Birthdays*. I have all sorts of digital notes across my phone and laptop. Some are single words, others stray sentences. Things I've spotted in the street, or weird little news stories I've read. There are paragraphs and pages, some of which might eventually become a story; others will never see the light of day. It would have come from there somewhere.

I do know it was in 2014, when I'd been a full-time writer for a year. A lot had changed in my life in a comparatively short period. I'd left a job I really loved and drifted away from colleagues with whom I'd enjoyed a lot of good times. It meant spending a lot more time by myself. I do have a sense of perspective. I'm not comparing it to night shifts down a mine, or sitting in a tank while navigating IED-riddled roads. I know I'm lucky – but it was a big change.

Without meaning to, it meant a lot of time for me to think about life and who I was as a person. I suppose that's where *Ten Birthdays* comes from.

I've written crime books and fantasy novels. Stories in which there are heroes and villains, life-changing events and (hopefully) unexpected twists. I think I reached a point where I wanted to write about life itself, where being 'the glue', as Neil calls it in the story, is something to celebrate. Where friendship is a character in its own right.

As a writer, all characters end up being my babies. Whether it's my crime books with Jessica or Andrew, Silver in my fantasy trilogy, or any of the others, they are always a part of me.

Good or bad, Poppy is probably the truest character to my own self that I've ever written. It took me more than two years of working around other things to get this story into the state it is now. I'm not sure I'll ever quite leave her where she is. Purley is not like the Somerset town where I grew up but Poppy's thoughts towards it are my own. I've not lived there in a long time but that leafy little place will always be home.

There are lots of little things throughout this that actually happened to me. You can guess at what you think is real and what's made up. It's strange to go from a little town that feels like the centre of the universe to then find out there's a big, wide world out there.

If you're curious, the places I wrote about in Toronto are all there... or they were. I would recommend Rasta Pasta – and the bakery opposite CTV on Queen Street. I think it's called Café Crepe.

I hope you enjoyed the book. Please do leave a review. There's no better way to help an author than to spread the word about something you liked. If you ever see me in a pub somewhere, I'll buy you a pint. Promise. As long as it's not some trendy wine bar in London. Have you *seen* the prices in those places?

Lots of thanks to Nicola, Claire and Gabby for all their work in making this better. Little things go a long way.

If you'd like to contact me, I'm always reachable through @kerrywk on Twitter or kerrywilkinson.com. And you can sign up to my newsletter www.bookouture.com/kerry-wilkinson to be contacted whenever I have a new book out.

Cheers for reading,

Kerry

Ten Birthdays Q&A

Kaisha from The Writing Garnet | thewritinggarnet.wordpress.com/

At the age of 16, Poppy's life began to take shape and her personality began to flower; thinking back to how you were at 16 compared to now, what advice would you give your younger self?

When you're 16, everything *feels* so important. Small disappointments are like the end of the world and anyone suggesting differently is instantly someone who doesn›t understand what it›s like. It›s a really hard age to be.

Adults can be dismissive – 'Oh, he or she is only 16' – and yet you're too old to mix much with kids who are even a couple of years younger. You're not old enough to vote, your views and opinions may often be ignored – and yet you're expected to make decisions that you're told will affect the rest of your life.

It's an odd limbo in which 16-year-olds are too young to work and earn a decent amount of their own money but too old to spend an afternoon playing at a friend's house. It's hard to feel stuck between two worlds. Then you throw in pressure of exams, the inability to get anywhere without a car, burgeoning feelings of love and sex, and so on... It's so, so difficult to be that age.

Because of that, it'd be hard to tell myself anything. I'd want to say not to worry. That everything works out. That I should be nicer to the people around me because, in the end, that's how people will remember you. That there's a big world and that petty arguments over nothing are such a waste of life. I doubt I'd listen to myself.

Erica Kelly from North of Normal Book Reviews | www.northofnormalbookreviews.com

I loved the three friends and the bond they had as a threesome as well as the bond they shared when paired off. Throughout the story, I loved, hated, then again loved Freya. Where did you get your inspiration for Freya?

I think everyone knows somebody whose life seems to be in perpetual crisis. It's one drama after another and yet they seem oblivious to the fact that *they're* the constant in everything thats happening.

It's interesting that you loved, hated and then loved Freya because I think that's exactly how those people's friends view them. They like the *individual*, they don't like the constant upheaval. I think the inspiration was simply looking around and seeing how people are. Real life is rarely heroes and villains. There are a lot of shades of grey.

Donna from Donna's Book Blog | donnasbookblog.wordpress.com/

Are there any books in the pipeline similar to *Ten Birthdays* we can look forward to?

Sort of. There's a bit too much of me in *Ten Birthdays* to be able to write something overly similar. I do have a book out in spring 2018 about a 17-year-old who awakens in a river, coughing and spluttering. She has no memory of getting there and, because of a few things that happen to her, she thinks she might be dead... and yet somehow still alive.

It's almost a murder mystery in which the investigator is the 17-year-old, who also happens to be the victim. But, because she's 17, she has her own group of teenage friends, issues with parents and siblings, and so on. She lived a normal life before this so she has to try to go along with that, while also being wary of everyone around her because she thinks one of them might have attacked her.

Michelle from Much Loved Books | muchlovedbooks.blogspot.co.uk

What parts of Mark's move to Canada and Poppy's visit were inspired by your own experiences there?

Even in my earliest notes, there was going to be a chapter in which Mark had moved abroad and Poppy was visiting him. I'd loosely noted down New York, simply because I'd been a few times, knew the streets and areas, and so on. I thought I could make it authentic. Then, before I started writing properly, I visited Toronto and knew it was right for the story. I took photos and made notes about the places I'd seen and been in the city. I talked to people – strangers! – and it all came together.

Sue from Read Along With Sue | sueandherbooks.blogspot.co.uk/

This book is very different from the Jessica Daniel series and a very emotional journey. How did you get inside a young person's perspective?

I'm not sure if a young person's way of experiencing things is necessarily that different from someone who's older. On many occasions as adults we might ask ourselves the same things about whether we're making sensible choices, or if everything is going to work out all right. The difference is the maturity to deal with things that don't go as planned. The perspective that something good isn't the greatest thing ever and something bad isn't the worst.

I'd like to think the Poppy who's turning 25 in the final chapter isn't the same girl who was turning 16 in the first. She's gained a bit of that perspective. Perhaps her mother's letters helped with it.

Samina from Escape into Books | escapismfromreality.blogspot.co.uk/

How difficult is it to write about a girl's thoughts and feelings when you are of the opposite sex?

I think, at our cores, most people want similar things from life. Whether that's to live a contented, happy existence; to be loved and to love; to feel safe... and so on. I'm not sure gender makes much difference to that. That's not to say there aren't differences to the way men and women might approach things but I've always thought the men are from Mars thing is nonsense. I could have more in common with a woman from the opposite side of the planet than I do with a bloke who's my age and nationality that lives next door. A lot of the differences thrown up between men and women are clichés anyway. Individuals go about things in a different way to one another and gender is only a part of that.

Sean from Sean's Book Reviews | seansbookreviews.wordpress.com/

With your success in crime thrillers, what was your inspiration for *Ten Birthdays*?

I always find it a bit awkward to talk about – because other people think far more about this than I do. If I'm writing a crime book, it's simply because that's the idea I have at the time. It's the same with my Silver Blackthorn fantasy series, or this, or any of my standalones. I never worry too much about genres because, for me, it's about the characters anyway. I'll have an idea about a character and the situation in which they find themselves. *Ten Birthdays* came along because that was what was in my head at the time.